Quantum Entanglement: ONE

"I do not pray for these alone, but also for those who will believe in Me through their word; that they all may be one, as You, Father, are in Me, and I in You; that they also may be one in Us, that the world may believe that You sent Me. And the glory which You gave Me I have given them, that they may be one just as We are one: I in them, and You in Me; that they may be made perfect in one, and that the world may know that You have sent Me, and have loved them as You have loved Me."

— John 17: 20-23 NKJV

Quantum Entanglement: ONE

Kathleen L. Daw

Printed in the United States of America

First Printing, 2015

ISBN-10: 0692430385
ISBN-13: 9780692430385

Front Cover: Almond Tree in Bloom at Night, Anthony Dunn Photography
Back Cover: NASA Sunrise

i

DEDICATION

To the ONE who said "light be and it was."

CONTENTS

ACKNOWLEDGMENTS

To Dr. John L. Mastrogiovanni whose years of preaching and teaching gave me something new to think about. To Jennifer AlLee who did the first read through and proofing. To David Rhodes and Mark Pavlinac who gave some additional input at just the right moment. To my parents James and Eva Daw, my sister Diane and brother Stephen. To Pastor Karen Mastrogiovanni, my church family and friends who prayed and encouraged me through to the finish.

CHAPTER I

*It was dark, but there was no human eye there to
see the darkness. Dark, empty, silent, and lifeless. Then,
but it takes too long to say it - Light, Life exploded into
the dark emptiness. Every atom, molecule and particle
danced with joy. The universe had turned inside out.
The beginning and the end, the Alpha and Omega, had
paused and resumed. The End had begun. The
Beginning was on its way!*

*The two who would, did wait for those He loved to
come were there. It was no problem. They were, are, will
be waiting for the time. In time, it was difficult for them
not to dance away with the joy swirling around them!
But they were ever faithful even while time was passing
and no true life yet on the scene, just dust. It was star
dust, smart dust, but still just dust. Purpose? A long
forgotten dream buried within dry, dead sands; carried*

by whirlwinds of heat or trampled under foot. Abandoned, deserted, forsaken, and forgotten.

Then, change occurred. The Light's mighty Wave of Color moved through and charged the lifeless dust. The dead, the dry, the dusty blazed jewel-like, entangled in His Light and separated from the darkness. The Light and His lights were one in the land! The many colors of His Light became waves of living light: emerald green, ruby red, and sapphire blue. Charged from within, the prismatic colors sparkled, flamed and gleamed. Joined together, a beacon diamond white, they glowed and beamed to the lost, dying and dead in the land. As the entanglement grew, more of His light could show through. Soon the Full Spectrum flooded and flowed, north and south, left and right. The darkness filled with life as the waves of splendor transformed dust into Light. Soon others answered the call to colors and fell in love with the Glorious Son.

"Rise and shine" is the command because the Light and His colors are one.

An egg-shaped white car pulled into the parking lot of a typical Southern California outdoor mall. A clear blue sky and still warmth of an early February heat wave should encourage shoppers to get a quick start on the day's activities. Yet, on this Saturday, it looked oddly empty to the passengers sitting in the small car. But to six year old Gabriella Messenger the parking lot was already crowded. Almond trees, her favorite, filled the landscape and they were in full bloom. Gabby's father had told her almond trees were also "messengers." They were the first trees to respond to the new season of light which was coming. He said light carried energy that would wake the trees up and cause them to burst out with blossoms and fruit. "Then, " he said, "you will be able to play with the light. You can see, touch, smell and even eat the light." That's when the bag of almonds appeared. The lesson would be complete once her parents gave her almonds to eat. Sometimes even the chocolate covered version. For Gabby, almond trees were right up there with Santa Claus and the Easter Bunny. For a minute, she sat in the car watching countless blossoms begin an adventure by setting sail on a passing breeze. The parking lot's almond trees were already awake and active in the warm spring light. Usually this would be an irresistible invitation to Gabriella. It gave her joy to dance and twirl with the floating white flowers she loved. This activity somewhat worried her mother. It usually led to falling into, and rolling around with, the large clumps of blossoms swept into piles around the mall. Where there were almond blossoms there were usually bees and Gabriella had been stung many times. Still, her mother didn't have too much concern today. Quantum Man was here!

Her parents, though, were uncertain as they got

out of the car, stood and looked around. There were plenty of cars but no people. A few movie scenes flashed through her father's thoughts. Her mother wondered if the event's time had changed. Gabby had no doubts whatsoever. The small, slight figure, with long, dark hair jumped out of the car. The mirrors on the front of her Full Spectrum Quantum Girl suit blazed in the reflected glory of the now intense sunshine.

"There he is!" Gabby said with excitement.

She started to run to the far corner of the mall with the rainbow cape of her still too big bright green costume streaming out behind her. Immediately, Gabby's father took off running after his daughter. Mrs. Messenger relaxed once she saw the direction they were heading and knew her husband would catch Gabby with ease. The mall's large oak tree had a noisy, colorful group of children around it. This was the object of Gabriella's great attraction.

Mrs. Messenger joined the audience of seated children and standing parents, but it took a minute or so to find her husband. Since the sound level was pretty high, even outdoors, she decided to save her question for later. But he greeted her and said, "I told her never to do that again." Gabby's mom squeezed his arm with affection. They were always on the same page. Prayers for Gabby's protection were still their top priority. Their daughter was fearless, impetuous, and bright. She would figure out a logical and good reason why she should do it again.

At first, Gabby's location wasn't obvious. Amid the jumping, screaming, laughing explosion of colors which were Quantum Man's fans, one child was hard to see. It was like looking through a kaleidoscope with tiny, moving pieces of glass. The small bits of humanity in their Full Spectrum costumes moved and rotated in changing patterns of color. Each wore their own, personalized favorite color with the official iridescent Quantum Man Cape. And each had a breastplate of faceted, jewel-like mirrors which reflected any light in a fabulous display. The shifting colors of the capes and the mirrored breastplates shining in the morning sun was a sea of color and light. It was easy to believe the Full Spectrum was invisible to the forces of evil who opposed Quantum Man. In fact, Net Man's Full Spectrum counterfeit, The Network, had already been "blinded by the Light." To the shear joy and undivided unity of the Full Spectrum in the audience and their kid actor counterparts on the stage. As an Alpha Force the special RGB Teams had rushed in. Although clothed in brilliant red, green and blue they would be invisible to the Netmen until Quantum Man wanted them to be visible. They had identified the Netmen and made the Network's activities obvious to all. Soon, as expected, Quantum

Man and his Quantum Pairs had arrived simultaneously. All the Pairs had swung into action with Quantum Man to save a little red haired boy who had almost been netted and cloned by the Network. But the rainbow wave of the Full Spectrum had overtaken and entangled Net Man's intended victim. The unlimited power of the "Bow Shock" and Quantum Man had separated them from their prey. Then The Network had to disappear into the outer darkness of the heavy netting at the edge of the stage. The light lacking, dull, vague and dark, muddy colors of their costumes made them virtually invisible.

Now came Gabriella's favorite part. Quantum Man would ask a few children if they wanted the entanglement with the Full Spectrum and himself to be permanent. and to become members. Unlike Net Man, Quantum Man would never force someone to become his Quantum Pair and part of the Full Spectrum. It had to be voluntary. The parents were always stunned by the sudden silence that fell on the audience. No matter how young, the children always replied to this scene as if their world hung in the balance. When a little boy or girl said "yes" the children celebrated as if they had seen the most wonderful event in their lives.

Gabriella was beside herself with excitement. More kids were now saved from the evil Net Man! She loved it and she knew, as a member of the Full Spectrum, she could do the same for someone someday. Her parents had been trying to tell her this was just a story and not real but, inside herself, she knew there was something real about it. It wasn't just a story. She knew it! People needed to be saved from evil before it was too late. They needed to have a chance to choose good, like the Full Spectrum did. Like Quantum Man did.

Now, seeing Net Man and his Network vanquished, Quantum Man stepped forward to talk to the kids. He was magnificent. Every color of the rainbow moved across his costume as he walked and the jewels on his breastplate seemed to be alive with color. It even impressed many of the parents and they were busy trying to figure out how those wonderful special effects had happened. The kids didn't analyze anything; they just accepted him for who he was: Quantum Man.

Quantum Man was wearing a stage mike and his voice cut through the general hubbub of the audience. "O.K. kids, repeat after me: Quantum Man believes in "All in One and One in All!"

A hundred young voices repeated: "All in One and One in All!"

Again Quantum Man asked: "If you're in trouble who will know it?!"

And again a hundred young voices answered:

"Quantum Man! Quantum Man!"

There was one more answer needed so Quantum Man asked: "And if Quantum Man needs help, who will know it?"

And the kids answered: "Me! Me!"

"Great answers Full Spectrum!" yelled Quantum Man. "And great support work, my Pairs. You've entangled another member of the Full Spectrum!"

When the cheering stopped the part of the Quantum Man show the parents especially loved had arrived. "Alright, Full Spectrum! And now it's time for our 'What's It Like to Be Me?' riddle so please give me your full attention. Remember, since we are entangled Light Writer will write the answer on your heart and you'll know exactly who or what the 'me' is. Are you ready, Full Spectrum?"

"Yes! Yes!" all the kids yelled.

"OK. Synchronize!" said Quantum Man and the results again were amazing as the kids quieted right down to listen to the clues of the riddle.

"What's it like to be me?" he said with drama. "Have you ever plunged through an emerald sea? Or flown through a sapphire blue sky soaring totally free? Felt yellow diamonds of glory pour over your head or washed in a river of fire from a love ruby red?

Remember, the light that bounces back is from the angle you see and all those colors, and more, are what it's like to be me."

Quantum Man stopped and gave the kids a couple of minutes to think. Then, pointing toward a tent and table at the right side of the platform, he said, "OK, Full Spectrum. When you've got the answer ask your parents if you can write it down on the Qubit Message Pad at the Quantum Computer Booth. Don't forget to leave your name, address and phone number-IF your parents give you permission. I know you'll all get the prize because we are synchronized!"

Quantum Man received a signal from the left of the stage by someone pointing at his watch. The cast had to start packing up so they could get to their next appearance on time. It was at a hospital a few miles away.

Illuminated by the noon sun, Quantum Man stepped up to the edge of the stage. His reflected glory definitely got the kids' attention but he had sad news. "We have to leave now."

Disappointed kids and relieved parents let out a collective sigh.

Quantum Man called out with strength and enthusiasm. "But no matter how far you and I travel today we'll still be together because we are – What's the answer, Full Spectrum?"

The question restored the children's excitement. With the mirrors on their costumes almost as reflective as Quantum Man's, the children yelled out "One!"

Aware of the time, the cast began to leave the stage because they knew their star had the kids' full attention. Quantum Man just wanted to finish up the show's usual ending. He needed to get started preparing for the next performance which would happen right after lunch.

Turning his attention back to the kids, Quantum Man said, "So remember, where there is darkness-You are the light!"

The kids, having memorized these Full Spectrum truths, put all their heart into their answer: "We are the light!"

Quantum Man, eye on the clock, said: "So, to do great good it takes?"

And the kids, now retaking their vows to Quantum Man, said: "All of us together!"

Thinking about the logistics for the day's next two performances, Quantum Man said: "To defeat great evil what do we need?"

And the kids, overcoming their fears of Net Man and all he represented, said: "The Full Spectrum! Yeah!"

The show was complete and they were only a little behind in time. So Quantum Man said, "Well, that's it for now kids except for one thing: What does Quantum Man stand for?"

The kids, knowing they were pledging their lives and everything, said: "All in One and One in All!! Yeah!"

Quantum Man was already half off the stage. But he stopped and said, "So get out there and be a brilliant part of the Full Spectrum!"

The kids were more than eager to do anything Quantum Man would do so the final "Yeah!" was deafening in its enthusiastic and high pitched, agreement.

The stage under the large oak was empty by the time the cheering had died away and Quantum Man was in deep discussion with the director.

Gabriella was still excited. She had seen her hero and she knew the answer to the question. As per instructions, she immediately located her parents and informed them. The Messengers let Gabriella run a little ahead of them as they all went toward the Qubit

Booth. The show was over, the crowd dispersing and it was a great afternoon. A little running would help her get rid of all the energy she had accumulated during the program.

However, the show was not entirely finished. Simultaneously, across the country, Quantum Man events were going on. The casts for each consisted of actors recruited from the immediate area. A few local teenagers had been hired to play The Network Men. Bored, they decided to start teasing a younger actor playing the part of a Full Spectrum member. He was the kid brother of one of the older adolescent boys surrounding him and was feeling small and unprotected. He had no ally in his sibling. The older brother had decided tormenting the younger brother was a fine way for his friends and himself to relax. So he picked up his little brother and, laughing, tossed him to another guy in The Network. The younger brother expressed his displeasure by struggling and crying for help. But he was still tossed back and forth between The Network members.

This immediately got Gabriella's attention. It was an attack on one of the Full Spectrum! Looking around for help she saw Quantum Man talking to someone at the Qubit Booth. Springing into action she shouted, "Quantum Man, Quantum Man!" She knew Quantum Man would be there to help even before Gabriella herself could arrive. The brave heroine rushed right into the middle of the oblivious, laughing Network Men. She pulled the crying youngster away from the laughing villain who was holding him.

"Stop!" Gabriella said with all the authority she could muster. "The Light is here!"

The original victim took this opportunity to make his escape. But The Network Men, recognizing a new source of entertainment, decided to get into character. "We don't see any light?" said one.

"Where is it?" demanded another in his best villain voice.

"In us!" Gabriella said with courage.

"Who is 'us', Light Bulb?" said the leader of the pack.

"Quantum Man, the Full Spectrum, and me!" Gabriella said standing her ground.

"What a Dim Bulb you are, " said the pack leader as he grabbed Gabriella and prepared to continue their tossing game. "Look around. You are alone. Do you see Quantum Man or the Full Spectrum? It's just a show you dumb kid!"

Gabriella did look around. She didn't hear Quantum Man's voice telling this Network Man that he was lying or ordering him to set her down. It was true!

There was no other Full Spectrum Pair around and where was Quantum Man? He should have been here already, she thought. Then Gabriella finally saw Quantum Man. Oblivious to what was happening he was laughing and talking with - Net Man! Gabriella was stunned. So stunned, in fact, that she didn't even hear the voice of her father ordering a now intimidated 'bad guy' to "Put my daughter down!"

Mrs. Messenger picked up Gabriella and walked a little distance away while Mr. Messenger gave the whole Network a quiet talk. Gabriella didn't see them nodding their heads in answer to Mr. Messenger's questions. She didn't see them shaking her father's hand and apologizing to the child they had originally been tormenting. Looking over her mom's shoulder, Gabriella only saw Quantum Man still talking to Net Man and doing nothing to help.

Gabriella and her mom walked over to stand under one of the almond trees to wait for her father. Gabriella was dispirited, her cape dragging behind her. The white almond petals were swirling around her in the now strong, heat dispelling afternoon breeze. This usually would have cheered her up, hooked her curious mind and brought forth numerous questions. But not this time.

Gabriella's mother lifted her daughter up to sit beside her on the short wall surrounding the tree.

"Gabby," she said trying to soothe and discipline her uncharacteristically sad little girl. "I know you're upset and your dad and I are upset too. We're proud you wanted to help the little boy, but you should have come to us first. We would have intervened and stopped it. You've never done anything like that before and we don't want you to do it ever again. OK?" Hugging Gabby, and stroking her long, shiny hair. Mrs. Messenger looked up to see her husband approaching. With him was a small group of people carrying what looked like a camera and sound equipment.

"Honey, this is Raf Billetdoux, the reporter from KCBC and his crew. They saw what happened and would like to do a story on what Gabby did." Mr. Messenger spoke with some restraint.

"Well, Mr. Billetdoux I...," Mrs. Messenger began but stopped after realizing her husband was not sold on the idea.

"Please call me Raf," urged the reporter. "And please say you'll do it. I would like to know what happened myself." Raf continued to talk while unobtrusively signaling his crew to start recording. He didn't want to lose this story. "Perhaps you could tell me exactly what happened to Gabriella? We caught the event visually but weren't close enough to get the sound." Raf subtly moved so the Messengers would be facing the camera as they answered his questions.

"We came to see Quantum Man today because Gabriella loves him and wants to be just like him, " said Mrs. Messenger. Gabby moved slightly at that remark.

"Yes, exactly like him, " said Mr. Messenger. "Our little 'Woman of Light' thought she saw the Network Men attacking one of the Full Spectrum and came to the rescue." Gabriella took hold of her proud father's hand and hid her face in his pant leg.

Perfect, thought Raf and hoped his camera man was getting this. "I know the Network Men are the villains on the Quantum Man Show and the Full Spectrum are the heroes who work with Quantum Man. Beyond that I'm not sure of the details."

Mrs. Messenger was an expert on the show. She watched with Gabriella who always explained the important facts in great detail. "On the show, when The Network attacks, Quantum Man always knows and does something to stop them through the Full Spectrum. Together they have unlimited power to defeat the enemy. It's called the 'Bow Shock'. The separate colors of the rainbow reunite in one blinding, white flash of light and unlimited power."

Gabriella sniffed a little, still hiding her face. Mr. Messenger continued the story. "Gabby was walking away with us when the teenagers portraying the

Network Men started teasing one of the child actors in the show. Since he was a Full Spectrum member Gabby decided she had to do something." Mr. Messenger patted Gabriella's head as he spoke.

Raf nodded in agreement. "I noticed she was yelling at the actor playing Quantum Man as she ran to the rescue."

Looking at Gabriella with some concern Mrs. Messenger was the one to answer. "Naturally, none of the Full Spectrum go after the Network Men without Quantum Man. In fact, Quantum Man always knows beforehand and is already there to help them when they arrive at the emergency. The Full Spectrum also already knows what the emergency is and what to do about it before they get there. Light Writer has written in their hearts. So you understand it was confusing to Gabby when her hero didn't even appear to hear her. We've tried to explain the difference between acting and real life but she's young and I'm not sure she understands. "

Raf knelt down to ask Gabby a question, making sure his sensitive mike would it pick up. "Gabby, how do you feel? Did you understand what your parents told you?" he asked knowing the camera had a clear shot of the child.

"I should never run off without permission. I

should never do that again. And I won't!" Gabriella said in a voice which signaled to her parents that she was ready to cry.

Her father picked her up and set her down on his shoulders. From there, Gabriella had a good view of Quantum Man and Net Man. They were working and laughing together with the Network Men as they dismantled the stage.

"I won't!" Gabriella said and then burst into tears.

"Oh, Gabby." Her mother was still trying to console her inconsolable daughter. She turned to the waiting reporter and started to say, "I'm sorry Mr. Billetdoux but.... "

Impatient, the reporter interrupted her with, "Raf. Please call me Raf and please wait a minute. I'll be right back." He rushed to get the permissions form for them to finish signing. He only had Mr. Messenger's signature from the first incident but the rest of the form was blank. He'd forgotten he hadn't told them they were being recorded. At first, he had just wanted it as background information. Then it started to develop into an interview with footage he wanted to use.

"Look Honey, let's get Gabby home. She's really taking this hard for some reason. Standing around with us while we answer these questions all over again isn't helping, " said Mr. Messenger.

Mrs. Messenger smiled at her decisive husband and said, "Once again you've said exactly what I was thinking. Let's go home."

By the time Raf Billetdoux had the slip in his hand and turned around, the Messengers had gone.

An hour later, the Messenger's van pulled into the driveway of their small but pretty house. The neighbors always thought of places filled with light and warmth when they looked at the Messenger home.

"Wow, look at all these petals still stuck on the van," Mr. Messenger said. "I thought the drive home on the freeway would blow them all away. I'd better wash them off."

Mrs. Messenger was gently waking Gabriella up. She had finally fallen asleep in her car seat. "I'll take Gabby in, get her settled and then come out and help you. It will only take a minute so wait for me, " she said as she finally was able to get the still drowsy child out of the van.

Gabriella walked with her mother up to the house, dragging the Full Spectrum costume she had refused to wear home. She went into the living room with her mother right behind her.

"Honey, " she said. "Today didn't turn out the way

you expected and I know you felt sad for the little boy. But remember, he is OK and hopefully those older kids will never treat anyone else like that again. How about you? Do you feel OK, Gabby?"

"OK, " Gabriella said flatly.

Her mother bent down and gave her a hug. "Gabriella, your Dad and I are proud you wanted to help, but you're too young to just jump into that type of situation. You should have asked for help first."

"I did, " she said more to herself than her mother. She was still sure Light Writer had told her heart to help the little boy.

"To someone real, " her mom emphasized. "Not pretend."

Gabriella looked startled for a second and then, while trying hard not to cry, she glanced at the clock on the wall. It was a recreation of a Stauer 1779 Skeleton watch. Its entire mechanism was visible through a transparent crystal cover. Gabriella usually loved to check the time and watch how the clock's parts moved together so precisely.

"Oh, look, " her mother said, following her gaze. "It's almost time for Quantum Man to come on. You watch it. I'm going to help Daddy clean the van and then we'll get dinner." Her mother turned on the T.V.

and left the room.

Gabriella sat down on her favorite space pillow and picked up her favorite teddy bear. Dressed in a miniature Full Spectrum costume the trusting, furry face looked straight at her. Turning to the watch the T.V. screen she quickly removed the bear's costume. The early afternoon news, on right before the daily children's programming, was ending. News Anchor, Michael Tidings started to read the last story.

"And now, if you or your kids love the Man of Light, Quantum Man, here's a story to brighten up your day. You may have been one of the few people in town who didn't know Quantum Man was making a guest appearance at a local mall today. But, even for those who did know, there were a few unexpected surprises."

The anchor covered some of the highlights of the show before the video came on. The video showed one small figure in blue pulled away from the Net Man character holding him by another small figure in green. In the next scene, the slight hero in green was standing alone in the center of the surrounding Net Men. Reporter Raf Billetdoux's voice began describing what was happening. "The show was not quite over yet. Some of the guest villains started teasing one of the kid actors in the show. The kid failed to get away and needed help. And help arrived in the person of

Gabriella Messenger. Wearing her Quantum Man Full Spectrum Team costume, she rushed in to rescue the victim and became part of the action. Since the actor portraying Quantum Man didn't notice what was going on the kid's parents came to the rescue in the nick of time."

From the angle of the camera Gabriella could see Net Man point out what was happening to Quantum Man. They laughed a little, shook their heads and then went back to their conversation. Gabriella sat quietly on her pillow, clutching her teddy bear, while Raf asked her parents what had happened and why. It was strange to watch herself cry on T.V. while her parents explained why she loved Quantum Man and wanted to rescue the little boy. She was glad the little boy was safe. She was happy the Net Men didn't get him. Then the video showed Raf bending down to ask Gabby how she felt and she started crying again. While Raf was narrating the story, the video showed the camera panning around. It had captured what she had seen- Quantum Man and Net Man talking and laughing with each other. She didn't understand why it hurt so badly, but it did.

Gabriella stood straight up and said, "I shouldn't do it again. And I won't!" She had stopped listening to herself answering Raf's questions. So she didn't realize she was in perfect synchronization with herself on the T.V. and the answer she just gave the reporter. She took her teddy bear and went running off to her bedroom. Both their Full Spectrum uniforms were left crumpled up and abandoned on the floor.

Michael Tidings came back on camera. "Quantum Man's creator, Joshua Cross, gave the following response through his publicist after the incident became known to him." A lead in to another video clip of previous Quantum Man events played while he read the statement.

"Quantum Man appearances take place simultaneously all over the country, usually on the same weekend. The actors are from local theatrical agencies and have no direct connection with the Quantum Man comic strip or T.V. show. Mr. Cross immediately realized how upsetting this incident was to the child and her parents. He is trying to get in touch with them but, so far, without success. We would appreciate any information anyone may have to offer. In the meantime, Mr. Cross would like to apologize to all the children and parents who love Quantum Man. He promises steps will be taken to insure each future event will truly represent the values they've come to expect from Quantum Man. "

The camera came back to Michael Tidings as he spoke for the station. "If you recognize the parents and child from this story, please contact our newsroom. And, hey kid, don't give up! This old world will always need light shining in the darkness and we think you're a perfect candidate for the Full Spectrum! That's it for tonight. "

Michael Tidings left the studio and went to his office. Raf was waiting there with another man and they both stood up to greet the news anchor. Raf said, "Michael, I'd like you to meet Joshua Cross. "

"Mr. Cross, " the anchor said as he smiled and extended his hand. "I was just thinking about you. This story left me with questions I believe only you can answer."

"Please call me Joshua," the writer responded as he shook the offered hand and then sat down. "I thought that might be the case."

"Joshua came to the station himself so I asked him to stay, watch the story and speak with you afterward," Raf said beaming with relief. He hadn't forgotten the missing information on the permissions form.

Michael smiled with understanding. "Well, I want to thank you both. We thought you were out of town or we would have tried to interview you for the story."

"I am sorry," Joshua responded. "I was out of town. The production company did the press release. I only returned this afternoon. Their representatives invited me out so they could explain the situation over coffee. As it happened, the coffee shop was across from your studio. We also just happened to be there when a promo for your news broadcast came on mentioning the Quantum Man Event. I decided to come over and find out more about the incident and the child involved, if possible."

Raf turned to Michael and said "I explained to Joshua that what he saw in the the broadcast was pretty much all we know."

"So you definitely don't know any more about the child or the parents?" Joshua asked.

"Not yet," Michael said. "But we want to. For some reason I don't want to let this story go. Would you be willing to give us a detailed interview about Quantum Man's story?"

"Sure," Joshua immediately responded. "When do we start?"

Raf jumped up and said, "I'll take care of everything." And, true to his word, soon both men were sitting in the studio reserved for Michael Tidings' trademark one-on-one interviews.

The anchorman began the interview. "Please welcome Joshua Cross. He is the creator of the comic novel "Quantum Man" and the children's animated series based on it."

"Thank you for inviting me," Joshua responded.

Michael led out with, "Joshua, I know there are some members of our audience who are unfamiliar with Quantum Man's back story. Could you please explain who Quantum Man is and why he does what he does?"

"To do that, I'll have to go back to a story my mother told me when I was a child," Joshua stated. "And, if you don't mind, tell it the way she told it to me."

Michael laughed and said, "Yes, please do. It already sounds too fascinating to pass up."

Joshua smiled in return and started his story. "Once upon a time, once in time, there was a place called Shelter Island where everything was Wonderful and Normal. On this Island two electrons were bonded together. They entered a super-energy state of infinite light and power called Normal. It was planned that more and more electrons would be bonded together in this one place and become one in Normal. Everything was, is and would be Normal.

But there was one who was not Normal. This one fell away from Normal. Others followed. They formed a dark, static producing current flowing along the edges of Shelter Island, always attempting to disrupt Normal.

Dark Current approached the Island and looked for a way to come between the two as one in the One called Normal. A parasite, Dark Current could do nothing as long as the two remained bonded to each other and Normal. But finally, through a forbidden mechanism, the way was found. The two suddenly, like lightning, dropped down from Superradiance into Self Energy, a powerfully destructive state. Instead of being constant with each other and One with the Infinite Normal they became producers of self-fueled infinities. Each moved farther and farther away from Normal. Instead of Absolute Light they only had their own light distorted and dimmed by the flow of the Dark Current. Instead of being part of the harmonies of the Never-ending Light they found themselves in a dark emptiness filled with an unending, overwhelming static. For the first time they knew they were separate, alone and they were afraid."

Michael interrupted, "I hope this isn't how it ended."

"Oh no," Joshua said, still in the story. "Normal was the only One who could change this tragic situation. By deflecting the Dark Current which was flowing into the now unbonded ones, dimming their light and disordering their energy, Normal used the Lamb-Shift to re-Normalize all. They were now set free from Dark Current and could choose to be rebonded to himself and each other in preparation for the Final

Superradient Event to come. Then they and Normal would live happily ever after."

"Wow!" Michael exclaimed. "And did you understand it all?"

"Not at first," Joshua laughingly answered. "I think I got 'once upon a time' and 'happily ever after'. My picture of everything else changed every time she told it. But I loved hearing it. It's interesting though. I think the saddest part of the story may have had the biggest influence on my life."

"The saddest part?" Raf asked.

"Yes, she explained how some just continued on in the Dark Current flow although they didn't have to since all had been released. They would be alone and afraid forever." Joshua, stopped for a moment, then continued. "She told me to 'never go with the flow' and, if possible, always find a way to help others to shift out of it. I know her story became the foundation of the Quantum Man stories, especially when I came to know it in another form later."

"Another form?" Michael asked. "What was it and when..."

The loud voice of the News Director boomed over the stage P.A. System, "Michael, you're needed on the air. There's important breaking news coming in!"

"Hey, Joshua, I'm so sorry" Michael apologized as he stood up. "If you can't wait for me could you arrange for a better time with Raf so we can continue this interview. I don't want to miss a detail." With that he bolted towards the main studio.

Joshua and Raf spent another hour or so talking. After agreeing on a time for the future interview Joshua left. Raf waited for Michael to return.

"There's something about this story, Raf. Did you get more background on the Quantum Man character from the Joshua Cross representative? What are the details?"

Raf flipped open a printed copy of the notes he had taken at the meeting with the Joshua Cross publicist. "Well Quantum Man has unlimited power but he limits how he uses it on earth. He decided to work through the Full Spectrum. How much of his power is expressed through them is limited by how many of them are willing to come together in a Quantum Pairing with him. And it is only by free choice on their part. Light Writer communicates Quantum Man's values and instructions by writing them on the hearts of the Full Spectrum with Light. Light Writer is constantly with the Full Spectrum and helps them tunnel into areas the Network has occupied. Net Man originally had power delegated to him by Quantum Man."

"So Net Man used to work for Quantum Man?" Michael asked.

"Right," said Ray. "His name originally was "Light Bearer" and he was not supposed to exercise power for anyone except Quantum Man. But he broke the rule. Now his only power comes through those he can trap into his Network, which is a counterfeit of the Full Spectrum. He hates people because they can potentially become what he was. People who are neither in the Full Spectrum nor the Network are called Lamps."

"Ah," Michael responded. "So they can be "Light Bearers" too.

Raf nodded and said, "Right, so Net Man wants to make them his slaves. That way they will never be carriers of light for Quantum Man."

"But," Michael interjected. "They are called 'Lamps.' Wouldn't they have light?"

"Yeah, but something happened in the first episode," Raf said. "They used to be surrounded and filled with Quantum Man's Full Light. They enjoyed it and each other. Then Net Man started to talk to them. He told them Quantum Man's Full Light was Light Pollution and his Light was trespassing on their own. As they did seem to have a light of their own, they believed Net Man. He told them, if they put up a Light

Shield, their own beautiful light could shine out with great brilliance. That was what he had done and they could be just like him."

Michael stopped Raf and asked, "What light does Net Man have? From everything you've described he doesn't have any."

"Well, everything in the Universe comes from or has to have some of Quantum Man's Light to even exist. Net Man is almost down to nothing. He can't do much on his own. He needs to work through Lamps to have any authority or effect in Quantum Man's domain. But he hates it and them. So the Lamps didn't understand one important thing. The moment they started to listen to Net Man, their understanding started to darken. The more they listened, the dimmer they got. Eventually the small amount of light Net Man still has left looked absolutely beautiful. Through disuse, the Lamps' capacity for light becomes so small they think the dense darkness around them is protecting and shielding them. But it's a barrier to the Light they need."

Michael was looking out his office window. It was a beautiful, sunny day. "Shielding them from them from what?"

"I suppose from Quantum Man, if they still know he's around. But many don't even notice any of the

Light around them. A Lamp not filled with Quantum Man's Light can end up doing all the killing, stealing and destroying that Quantum Man is against. And that's without even directly participating in the Network. But it's a very attractive state of being and does make the Lamp an even better candidate to Net Man."

Michael started thinking about Gabriella but he asked, "How does Net Man work if he doesn't have any power?"

Looking at his notes, Raf answered, "Any Lamp, even the worst, has more light than Net Man but they are afraid of the dark. They were never meant to be in the dark. They were always meant to receive the unlimited power of Quantum Man and give his Full Light to the world. Net Man twists and uses their fear, making them think they need his light to survive. In reality, the only source of real power is Quantum Man. Net Man and the Network can't stand against the Bow Shock that occurs when the Full Spectrum joins together with Quantum Man as One. In actual fact, the Network Men have a hard time coming against even one color of the Spectrum, or Spectra. Quantum Man is always with each individual Spectra. Net Man's only weapon, in that case, is the same fear of the dark he uses with the unfilled Lamps. He tries to make it appear as if Quantum Man is not with him or her and doesn't care what happens to them."

"Can that happen?" Michael asked.

"Yes," Raf answered. "Net Man uses his Network to surround the Spectra with darkness and tries to block out all awareness of the Light. Net Man tries to make them believe Quantum Man can't see them in the dark; that he doesn't know where they are. Then they lose heart. They're still everything they always were. They are still part of the Full Spectrum. Quantum Man and Light Writer are still writing on their hearts – they just don't see it."

"And that's all it takes?" Michael asked.

"That's all it takes," Raf answered. "In fact, it's the same thing Net Man tells those he recruits. He tells them, if they become part of the dark he creates, they can hide and do anything they want. They are told this is because the light can't be present to reveal their dastardly deeds."

"Well, that's not true. Light is everywhere, visible or not." Michael said. "So Net Man lies to everyone?"

"Yeah, himself included." Raf answered.

Michael looked at him and asked, "This is kind of heavy stuff for a kid's show."

Raf nodded and said, "That's one of the most interesting things about it. Most of what I just told you is not stated flat out in the show. The kids get it at their level of understanding. But any adult watching should understand the true, ultimate nature of the conflict. A lot of adults watch this show." Raf glanced at the clock behind Michael's desk. "Man, look at the time. Do you mind if I get going? I've got to pick up tomorrow's schedule," Raf asked already heading for the door.

"OK, but keep trying to locate the kid and her family. See you tomorrow, Raf," Michael answered. He looked down at the written background notes on his desk. Somehow this story doesn't feel finished, he thought. I'd like to know how it ends. He called up the raw video of Raf's story and watched it again until the end. The camera caught the Messenger family as they walked away. A good breeze must have come up because even the trees were swaying. White petals were swirling everywhere and even obscured the family from the camera's view. "Huh, those trees almost look like they're dancing," Michael Tidings thought. "I love it!"

Net Man was ecstatic when he saw his chosen victim diverting from Quantum Man. He knew Light Writer could not work through any individual unless the exchange had happened. It wouldn't happen if he had anything to say about it. He saw Quantum Man's Color Force everywhere, limiting where and how he wanted to work. But Quantum Man could do nothing to stop Net Man if his individual target didn't agree to or, even better, know about the exchange. His disgust for Quantum Man was intense and overwhelming.

"What a fool he is to allow them all that freedom of action. Why he goes to all that trouble for these small bits of animated matter who don't realize their own weakness is beyond me. But," he laughed, "it does give me a way to hurt him! When I get through, I'll turn his Carbon Lamps into carbon cubes. They're block heads anyway." Glee over the success of his plans centered Net Man's attention back on himself. He failed to notice the small 'Lamb Shift' taking place. There'd been a change in the circumstances of the plan which had left his prey heartbroken and pale with sorrow. But all Net Man knew was he had won this battle!

Joshua stopped writing. He wasn't sure he used all the technical terms correctly in his strip. But he loved how they spoke to him and the ideas they let him describe. He'd check them later but now it was time to take a break. He turned the computer on and watched the recording he had made of today's news story. He was a little frustrated because they had not been able to track down Gabriella and her family. So, he did what he did under every circumstance, he prayed:

"Lord, please help me find Gabriella and show me how to help her understand what happened today. Also send others that You know will lead her to You. Please turn what happened today into something which will become a to blessing her. Please protect her, Father. Thank you."

Joshua got up to go to the kitchen. But then he remembered the message he'd received to call Michael Tidings, the KCBC reporter. I'll probably have to just leave a message since it was so late, he thought. He turned around and walked toward the phone.

CHAPTER 2

Joshua hung up the phone after speaking with Michael Tidings. He had just finished telling him he'd go over to Mountain View College today and check out some information for him. The events of nine years ago had been the beginning of a strong and fruitful friendship for the two men. It had begun with the, so far, unsuccessful search for the little girl whose plight had so captured their attention. Gabriella must be a teenager now, Joshua thought, but neither he nor Michael had, or would, give up. This tenacity combined with common faith and heart interests had forged an unbreakable bond. Joshua had been working on a story when Michael called and went back to it after they'd hung up. There was no rush, Michael had said. But Joshua stopped and stood up. He felt a sudden sense of urgency to get to Mountain View. Maybe Michael's going to need the information sooner than he expected. I better get over there. With that thought he grabbed his car keys and rushed out.

"Quantum Man was waiting for what he knew was coming. Two of the Full Spectrum were heading into danger although they were not yet aware of it. Net Man's plotting and planning was about to pay off. He had found a way to net more victims and plug them into his Network. It would be costly and destructive. But he was, as he so often said, 'OK with that.' Quantum Man knew the price to stop that villain would be high. It broke his heart but he'd made sure he was the first line of defense. The first member of the Full Spectrum had arrived and now..."

At a special outdoor event a young woman was patiently sitting among an audience of 50 to 60 people. Well, patiently for her so there was a little foot tapping and the occasional sigh. But the beautiful Southern California early spring morning made the wait endurable. After raining during the night the winds had briskly moved the rain clouds out of the area. Now the sunshine was warm and the air clean, fresh and filled with fragrant, swirling blossoms. In fact, sitting outdoors in the middle of the sunny campus at the C.S. Rockwell School of the Arts wasn't all bad. It had given sixteen year old Gabriella Messenger some unexpected entertainment. She was observing the relaxed happiness of her companions. Some other advanced science students might have looked around and thought about seals basking on a warm beach. Or maybe even a study on the psychology of pleasure and pain. But not Gabriella. Before coming she had just read an article describing the weight of a human being as being equal to about 100 billion dust particles. Looking at the collection of human beings around her she started to calculate. There are 100 trillion cells in an average human body and 100 trillion atoms in each ordinary human cell. The passing breeze triggered a chain reaction of smiles, deep breaths and reaching out for elusive flowers. She thought it was odd.

"What is it that 'feels' and 'enjoys'?" she asked herself, already drifting farther and farther into her imagination. "Do the atoms themselves 'feel' the movement?" Collections of atoms experiencing the movement of another mass of atoms as a comforting pleasure was odd.

Everyone around her was starting to become more and more indistinct. She saw them with larger and larger spaces between each of their atoms. The waves or particles of the light they were sitting in could then pass freely through.

"Why would that be a pleasure and not just an experience? In fact, why would...," she would have continued her thought but a voice from the podium interrupted her thoughts.

Michael Tidings, well-known and well-respected

news anchor had just been introduced. The last ten years had only added a mature confidence to the air of friendly interest he always projected. Both the audience and media people covering this small but interesting event perked up. Whatever the news, when Michael Tidings spoke, you expected it to be worth listening to.

"Welcome to all you friends of Joshua Cross." He began. "I was proud to have counted myself among you for the last nine years. As you may or may not know, a story my station did on Quantum Man ten years ago brought us together. And, once you got to know Joshua and became his friend, your family became his family and your causes his causes." He paused and took a drink of water before continuing to speak. As he looked out at the audience he happened to catch a flash of anger and something else cross a young woman's face. His newsman's instinct registered and filed it away for possible future investigation. "But we are here today to deliver some good news for all you friends of Joshua Cross and Quantum Man fans. Joshua was the sole creator of Quantum Man. After his death during a bizarre accident last year, it was feared the cartoon strip had come to an end. But we're here to celebrate the good news Joshua left in his last will and testament. All rights to the comic strip are to be awarded to the young person whose life and dreams embody the Quantum Man vision. We are here today to announce the winner of the world-wide contest which was held to find just such a young person. The winner is a local teenager. Please welcome 16 year old Peter Lux!"

Everyone broke into applause and cheers, especially Gabriella. Peter and she had been friends since they both started attending a pre-school for gifted children. And they were still closer than many brothers and sisters. Gabriella had gravitated toward science and Peter toward the arts. They fought each other's battles as often as they fought with each other. They often dueled I.Q. to I.Q. for hours. Then they'd finish up the discussion by laughing themselves silly over an old Abbot and Costello movie.

The tall, lanky Peter looked more like a basketball player than an artist as he approached the microphone. "I just want to say, 'God rocks!' I had two dreams for my life but I wasn't sure how they could come true. One was being able to attend the C.S. Rockwell School of the Arts. The scholarship which is a part of this award will allow me to come here. The other was to meet and work with Joshua Cross, Quantum Man's creator. When he died I thought that dream was over. But now I have the opportunity to carry his work on into the future. It just proves how absolutely nothing is impossible with God!"

The assembled faculty, friends and family broke

out into loud applause. All except one, Michael Tidings noted as he stepped back up to the podium. "And I think that's the right way to end today's event. Remember what Peter accomplished today. And remember, if you have the vision, nothing is impossible! Go out and do the impossible!"

Gabriella waited while Peter was greeted and hugged and interviewed. She couldn't be prouder if it had been happening to herself but she couldn't say she was happy.

Finally Peter was free to come over to his waiting friend. "Wow, Gabby, I didn't think this would become some kind of media event. Do you think they'll broadcast everything I said!" He was still excited.

"For your sake, I sure hope they don't!" Gabriella said in a joking tone. "But, congratulations! You must be flying!"

Peter jokingly nudged her arm. He knew a diversion when he heard one. "Yeah, it's like God read my Christmas list and gave me everything I asked for – only even better!"

Gabriella countered with practicality. "I think it's because you are smart and talented but whatever you want to believe is O.K. with me."

Peter counter attacked with facts. "Gabby,

thousands of people sent in their applications and projects. They were great! I was kinda surprised I got it. It was pretty miraculous!"

Gabriella signed and shook her head, "You know Peter, you have no self-confidence. Why you would want to waste all that high I.Q. of yours on some cartoon instead of doing something important I will never understand."

Peter understood why his friend felt the way she did but he didn't feel like fencing today, of all days. "Gabby," he said, "I don't want to argue. This is a great thing for me and I feel I'm going to be doing what God created me to do!"

Gabriella felt all her frustration of not being able to sway her friend from the "dark side" of superstition and ignorance. Today had made her see it was hopeless so she heatedly responded, "You just proved my point. You can't think for yourself!"

Peter hesitated for a minute so he wouldn't yell back at his friend the way he wanted to do. "Look, you don't have to agree with me. I just wanted to give you one of the T-Shirts they made with my version of the cartoon on it."

Gabriella took a few steps away, not quite sure why she was so angry. "Quantum Man! Thanks but no thanks. You know how I feel about that fake. It's just a lousy cartoon-but, hey, I know you'll make it better. If any one can. Look, I'm late and I've got to finish moving my stuff over to the dorm at Mountain View. I don't want the college to think they've made a mistake letting some disorganized kid in too early."

Peter looked at the refused shirt for a second. Then he pushed aside his hurt feelings, not completely sure of why he was so angry. "O.K. Gabby, and don't worry, you'll be the smartest one there even if you are one of the youngest students they've ever let in. I'll be praying for you. And, hey, you're coming over for the celebratory Matrix Marathon tonight aren't you?"

They were both relieved when Gabriella said, "Uh, sure, thanks Peter. I'll see you later."

Peter watched her walk away with some concern. After entering Mountain View College Gabriella had less and less tolerance for Peter's faith. She acted as if she believed Peter's future was in danger if he continued on the way he had chosen. This was ironic because Peter had similar fears for Gabriella. He didn't want her to be lost in any sense of the word.

A familiar voice interrupted this anxious line of thinking. "Good friend of yours, Peter?" said Michael Tidings in a concerned, and irresistible, tone.

"The best," said Peter. "She's more like my sister though."

"I noticed her earlier," the anchorman said still thinking his observations through. "What's her name, if I may ask?"

Peter absently answered, "Gabriella Messenger." He was already moving toward his family who were waving him over. "I'm sorry, Mr. Tidings. My family is trying to get my attention. If it's O.K. I have to run."

Taking silence as agreement he took off running. The stunned anchorman was left staring at the rapidly disappearing figure of Peter's friend. "Gabriella Messenger," said the famous voice, not even realizing he had said it out loud. As if to make sure all his memories came back, the breeze had strengthened and started to blow a number of fallen blossoms around. They swirled up after Gabriella had passed and completely obscured her from sight. "Quantum Man!" he said so excitedly that he startled a few by-passers. KCBC had broadcast the story of Quantum Man creator Joshua Cross and his sudden death. It featured the final frame of the last comic strip he had drawn. It showed Quantum Man and the Full Spectrum standing together and surrounded by a deep darkness. Quantum Man was holding the wonderfully colorful capes of two fallen members of the Full Spectrum. It was obvious they were mourning the loss of their two friends. But the darkness could not overcome the combined presence of Quantum Man and his Spectrum. They filled the location with a brilliant and intense white light. Through the light others could be seen looking. Some were attracted and some repelled. On either side of Quantum Man were two figures. They were so brightly illuminated the more natural light surrounding them looked like a jet black outline. To their right and left were the two Full Spectrum characters being cut from the comic strip storyline. Bright smiles were on their faces and their hands raised in farewell. The caption read: "Arise, shine..." The reaction was mixed. Some called it ironic how this was the last thing he had drawn for the strip. Others called it prophetic. Michael Tidings knew which it was. Smiling and laughing at himself, he went off in search of Peter Lux and the end of the story. He thought.

CHAPTER 3

Peter sat back from his computer and chewed on a pencil. This was his first story for the Quantum Man cartoon strip. He wanted to continue the story from where Joshua left off. He felt it was somehow important and there were questions which needed to be answered for the fans. And me, too, he thought.

"The beach head was established. It was once a place claiming it stood for, and with, Quantum Man but the Network had also been there for years. Now the number of those ensnared had grown to the point where Net Man's influence was becoming visible. Despite that, there still others trying to work there who were not a part of the Network. In fact, over the years, building maintenance had received many calls from a constant stream of newcomers. The callers talked about the

47

dimness of the office light. They also had questions about an obscure, imperceptible mist that always felt as if it was hovering in front of their eyes. Then there were all the complaints of 'How gloomy it always seemed' yet nobody could seem to figure out why. Now only the hardiest, or most stubborn, were still trying to work in the darkness which encompassed them. An unnatural, hyper-illumination existed within the deepening darkness. It was created by the unseen polarization of the two sides. The source of the limited, ever fluctuating light was the Network. The induced glare began to spread stress, headaches, and even increasing blood pressure. And productivity and efficiency fell in almost equal proportions. For the Network it was becoming more comfortable and familiar since, for them, full light was intolerable. Even the dimmest light source made it hard for them to see their work and gave them headaches. And, at least for the moment, they were basking in Net Man's pleasure. He had come up with a foolproof plan to forcibly recruit new members and it had been working spectacularly well!

Of course those two Full Spectrum light polluters almost blew it though. As soon as they showed up the Network realized their instinctive photophobia was well-founded. The Full Spectrum began to make a remark here or point out something there. Certain intended victims began to blink their eyes as if waking up and started to look as if they could see what was going on.

But the Network stopped that nonsense. 'Yeah,' they all agreed. 'We put their lamps out, didn't we!' Not all of course. They had to get rid of some of the others too because the light had just flowed in and illuminated them. Oh, well. No great loss. There were many more where those had come from."

The office of Dr. Lumière Adversier was as exceptional and unusual as Dr. Adversier himself. It had a dim coolness about it even in the hottest weather. Unlike the offices of most of the professors at Mountain View, it looked spacious, even large. It was uncluttered by the piles of books, papers and personal mementos found in most of the other offices on campus. The furniture was sleek, modern and somewhat uncomfortable. As Gabriella could attest to from personal experience. He was her faculty advisor. But Dr. Adversier liked people to state their business and then get out and get to work. So Gabriella Messenger, now a doctoral graduate student, hadn't had too many long talks with him.

At least not sitting on this miserable chair! A thought that didn't comfort her as she twitched around trying to find a comfortable spot. She was there to help Dr. Adversier with some interviews. But first the doctor wanted her to watch a video of a school press conference and news story from a couple of days before. The KCBC anchor covering the story was Angelique Tidings. She happened to be the daughter of the former station anchor, Michael Tidings. But she had stepped into the position based on her own qualifications after the death of her father. The well respected news veteran had died in a freak accident along with KCBC reporter Raf Billetdoux. They had been covering a story together. As beautiful as he had been handsome she also had the same open and compelling personality. But the similarities didn't end there. She was already getting the reputation of being an excellent investigative reporter. Like her father, Angelique recognized when an obscure anecdote might be the tip of a potential iceberg of a story. A few modern day 'Titanics' had been prevented from running aground and sinking with all hands on board by her broadcasts. A video showing the beautiful Spanish style Mountain View campus was on the green screen behind her as she spoke. It showed various well known campus sites. Then there was a close up of the school motto carved in stone over the door of the administration building.

As usual, the anchor was explaining the story in a voice which made you want to listen to what was said. "The battle over the school motto of Mountain View Institute of Technology is over. It was decided today in favor of those wanting change. Founded as a training school for Christian ministers the Mountain View motto was from the Book of Romans in the Bible. The quote was 'We being many, are one body in Christ, and every one members one of another'. The wording on the new seal will state: 'We being many, are one body.' Dr. Lumière Adversier, Board Member and Head of the Physics Department, gave the explanation for the change. Your KCBC was there."

The video focused on the dignified and coolly matter of fact Dr. Adversier. The site was in the large meeting room where most of the traditional or important events of the school happened. He was standing in front of a massive, old fireplace. Above him, over the mantle, the new motto had already replaced the original version. It was so efficiently done no one could have guessed anything else had ever been there. Anyone well acquainted with the doctor was not surprised.

The doctor himself was pleased indeed and said, "This is a great day for the Mountain View Institute of Technology. We honor the foundation of the past. The excellence of this international and all inclusive institution has been built on it. But we will be moving on into an even more glorious future. We want to welcome and embrace the world-wide diversity of ideas and concepts. This will help us create and fulfill the scientific visions of tomorrow."

The sound bite ended and the camera was back live with the station anchor. "What we just heard is a good reminder of how the visions of tomorrow are on their way. What part will you play in the vision of the future? Or, perhaps a better question we should ask ourselves is which vision of the future is the one you will be a part of? Well, that's it for tonight." Angelique Tidings signed off with a smile and her father's signature tag line.

Only the tapping of his pen on the clear, shining top of his desk indicated the frustration the professor felt in his moment of triumph. "Reporters. Always have to add their own spin on a story," he said with only a slight increase of emotion in his pleasant and well modulated voice.

Gabriella was not so stoic. "Tell me about it! I've been watching this particular anchor for the last five years. I always feel she's implying something but I'm not sure what it is," she spoke with her usual fervor. "Since she's not one of Mountain View's alumni, I can't guess the specifics of what is bugging her this time."

Although she was wondering if some of those former students had gone to Tidings with their grievances. Dr. Adversier had assigned Gabriella to explain to the alumni why the school motto needed to be changed. Gabriella was good with people and often fulfilled the role of troubleshooter for her mentor. She had warmth and the human touch which usually soothed and won over those alienated by Dr. Adversier's cold resolve. Many of the alumni Gabriella had spoken to now saw the change as a timely move in the school's future expansion. But many others, although they liked Gabriella, had remained unmoved. Maybe they were the sources for the anchor's story.

Dr. Adversier's voice broke into Gabriella's unhappy reflections. "I'm sure I know what Ms. Tidings is driving at. I'll tell you about it some day. But there are more important things to do. Do you have the files for the last two first responders you recruited?" The tone of his voice meant the subject was now changed.

"Yes, I do," Gabriella said while handing over the two files she had brought in to Dr. Adversier.

The doctor didn't bother to look at the files. He knew if Gabriella had prepared them they were up to his standard requirements. So he just put them down on his desk and said, "Alright, please bring the first one in if you will."

Gabriella walked out of the office and brought back Lt. David Harbinger. He was wearing a well-cut business suit for the interview. But he still carried himself as if he was in the marine uniform he had been proud to wear for so many years. Neither smiling nor frowning, Dr. Adversier stayed seated behind his desk. But did extend his hand to the lieutenant for a quick handshake. Gabriella motioned to the two chairs opposite the empty expanse of the desk and handed Lt. Harbinger a form as he took one of the seats.

"Thank you for returning for a second interview, Lt. Harbinger." Dr. Adversier said in a voice neither warm nor cold. It was also still impossible to tell from his expression whether he was glad to see the lieutenant or not.

The lieutenant was a good match for the doctor. He said, "This opportunity is one anybody would love to take part in. I'm happy to be here." But yet he gave nothing away in voice or body language as to the truth of his statement.

Gabriella, smiling and nodding at the lieutenant's remark. She was the only person in the room who looked pleased. But it was Dr. Adversier who said, "I'm satisfied you feel that way. And of course you know my assistant, Ms. Gabriella Messenger."

At that the lieutenant turned to Gabriella, smiled and said, "Yes, sir. We met at the first interview. Ms. Messenger gave me a comprehensive explanation of what this program involves. She encouraged me to see all the new developments and advancements which could result from this type of project. It sounds as if you are building something revolutionary. It will change how first responders will function in the future and I would love to get in on the ground floor."

Then a smile did cross Dr. Adversier's face. Once again Gabriella had effectively delivered the message. The doctor nodded to Gabriella and gave her a pleasant look. "We've already covered your experiences in the military and your last five years as a paramedic. Now, there are just a few more questions I need to ask you and I must give you some information. This is a politically correct and litigious time. So the following questions are not ones asked in a job interview. But this is a new and revolutionary technology and, due to our recent experiences, I must be blunt. The truth of your answers could be a matter of life and death should you become an active participant in the program. Please look over the consent form that Ms. Messenger handed you. Sign it if you are willing to answer these confidential questions. If you are not willing, then please accept our thanks for your time. We would not be able to go further in considering you for this position."

Lt. Harbinger studied Dr. Adversier and the form with an impassive look which was yet focused and piercing. Then he signed it. "I wouldn't let a few personal questions keep me from participating in such a milestone of human advancement."

Dr. Adversier once again congratulated himself. As usual, putting Gabriella in charge of the search for suitable personnel had been profitable. "Splendid, splendid. You are especially well qualified and I also would not want you to miss out. Now for my first question. Would you be willing to take a battery of tests where most of the questions will deal with your religious background and beliefs?"

Both Gabriella and the lieutenant were surprised at the question. The lieutenant covered his reaction better and quicker. "Of course Dr. Adversier but perhaps I should tell you up front I'm not religious at all. I may be more of an agnostic than an atheist but religion doesn't figure at all in my life or life choices. If that disqualifies me then I wouldn't want you to waste any more of your time." His response was in the matter of fact and blunt way he approached all decisions which were ultimately in someone else's hands.

Gabriella looked at Dr. Adversier, interested to see what his answer would be. "Oh, no, no," Dr. Adversier said, standing up and sounding positive and pleased. "Just take the tests if you will and don't worry about it. I'm optimistic. I have an expectation the results will match up well with your professional experience. Ms. Messenger, please see Lt. Harbinger out and bring in the next candidate."

"Thank you for your time, sir," the lieutenant said as he stood up. He shook hands with the doctor and left with Gabriella.

Gabriella handed over Lt. Harbinger to the doctor's waiting secretary. Then she turned to greet the second applicant of the morning. This was Sean Lewis, a wild looking young guy all in basic black. His hair was spiked and in two colors completely different from the colors Gabriella had seen him wearing the last time they had met. His ensemble was finished off by a couple of painful looking pieces of jewelry in his ears and nose. A few years younger than Lt. Harbinger he was quick to express his emotions. And, as Gabriella could, he was also quick to pick up on the reactions of others.

Sean's eyes and smile were full of amusement when he said, "Don't worry, Gabby, it's all temporary. Being all things to all men, at least for this morning."

Gabriella shook his hand and laughed apologetically. "I'm sorry I was so obvious, Sean. It just looks extremely painful. Let me take you in to see Dr. Adversier."

Both walked into the office smiling. The doctor neither smiled nor stood up but extended his hand and motioned to the chair directly across from himself. As she did before, Gabriella moved to pick up a release form but Dr. Adversier kept his hand on the forms. Sensing a slight change in the atmosphere, and feeling a little confused, she sat down and tried to discern her boss's subtle expression of emotions. This reaction to the young paramedic was not the reaction she had expected from the him and she couldn't account for it.

Dr. Adversier kindly said, "Mr. Lewis, thank you for coming to our second interview. Especially since I know you had short notice."

The affable and unflappable Mr. Lewis replied, "Yes sir. I understood from Gabby you needed to make the decision today and I apologize for showing up in my alter ego disguise. It's wouldn't be my first choice for a job interview."

Maybe that was it Gabriella thought. Sean was incredibly observant and aware of the people around him. "I hoped I had set your mind at rest, Sean," Gabriella interjected. "Dr. Adversier said not to worry about it." She look to Dr. Adversier for corroboration of their previous conversation.

The slightest flicker of disapproval disturbed the doctor's pleasant smile but it was now back in place. "Yes, Ms. Messenger is quite correct Mr. Lewis," he said with an emphasis on the use of their full names. "You're not applying to the Fashion Institute. Besides, I thought it would give me a much better idea of what you superheroes do in your spare time. In this day and age, I know phone booths are hard to find."

At that Sean Lewis laughed outright. "For paramedics, sometimes being able to turn into a superhero with superpowers would be great. But, if what I hear about this program is even half true, it sounds as if you've created a phone booth a superman wouldn't be ashamed to use."

The doctor loved hearing the program praised. Gabriella anticipated the comment would break this odd restraint on the his part.

The doctor continued to smile but it didn't quite reach his eyes. He said, "I'm hoping many first responders will agree with you. My impression from your resume and the first interview Ms. Messenger conducted is that you are a busy man. For example, I know you were at work last night and into the wee hours of this morning. Where were you off to before our interview?" the doctor inquired looking at his notes.

Now Sean was in his element and was happy to explain, "Every Saturday morning the men in my church meet with at risk youth. We have breakfast together and often go to a sports event or on a special field trip. Today, I just stayed for the breakfast and then rushed over here. This used to be my personal version of camouflage and it still helps me put some of the kids at ease before they get to know me better. Since you had mercy on me, I was able to stay until the breakfast was finished. So, thanks again."

Dr. Adversier smiled then and stood up saying, "Think nothing of it. As I said before, for these positions, it's not the clothes that will count. Look, I know you must be exhausted so I won't keep lobbing questions at you. If you stop by my secretary's desk, she'll give you a packet of tests to take home and bring back after you finish them. And as soon as possible, please."

Gabriella had thought Sean's personal warmth was dispelling the chill in the conversation. This was the second surprise. She stood up wondering why the doctor was ending the interview so unexpectedly.

"Thank you both for your time. I enjoyed meeting you, Dr. Adversier. I hope we'll have an opportunity to work together." Sean extended his hand for a friendly handshake with both Gabriella and the doctor.

"Glad you could get here, Sean, and hope to see you again soon. Get some rest!" Gabriella said as she moved to see the departing paramedic out. When she returned she found the doctor in what passed, in him, for high spirits.

"Wonderful, Ms. Messenger! I knew you were the one for this job. It was a good afternoon's work. I believe we have found the one who completes our first team."

Gabriella decided to test the waters and said,

"Thank you, Dr. Adversier. So, would you like me to set up all the paperwork for Sean Lewis when he returns his tests?"

Now it was the doctor's turn to look taken aback, if only for a second. "Sean Lewis! No of course not. Lt. Harbinger is the one I mean. Why would you even suggest Mr. Lewis as our choice after the results of this interview?"

Now Gabriella was confused again. "I know both the lieutenant's and Sean's credentials as paramedics are equally tremendous. But I thought Sean's personality might work better with a team facing such high stress conditions. And you did say his appearance wouldn't be held against him."

Dr. Adversier laughed outright. "Hold it against him? By no means. Mr. Lewis obviously has little respect for the demands of formal social interactions. His appearance gave me hope he might be perfect for the job. He looked tough and maybe a little reckless."

Gabriella had checked into the ministry Sean Lewis was helping. She also had several long conversations with him during the search process. "Tough and reckless" was not how she would describe the young paramedic. "Well, I'd call him strong but the clothes are only camouflage for working with the kids at his church. It lets them see he knows where they're coming from."

Dr. Adversier was shaking his head at Gabriella and looking incredulous at what he'd just heard. "Oh, he's well-camouflaged alright. In fact, I am a little surprised you didn't take this religious component of his life seriously. To be brutally frank, I feel it makes him not only soft-hearted but potentially soft-headed as well. I saw it as soon as he walked in the door."

Gabriella protested mildly. She had given the doctor a complete briefing on both candidates. "But sir, you knew he has done a lot of part-time work at his church for several years."

Dr. Adversier was amused now. "Ms. Messenger, I don't care if someone just attends a church or even works for one. It doesn't automatically make them a practitioner of the superstitions they are surrounded by. I'm amazed you were so prejudiced against Mr. Lewis. Of course, then there are those who never darken the door of a church. We can't assume they are intelligent, enlightened and free from a belief system one can only describe as medieval."

Gabriella was also somewhat enlightened now, "So that is why you wanted those tests done on Lt. Harbinger?"

Dr. Adversier was pleased he and his assistant were back on the same page. "Yes. The background checks on both Lt. Harbinger and Sean Lewis found a few things in their past which don't seem to be there now. I wanted to make sure these changes came from self-confidence and a healthy ego. Not through subservience to some religious obsession. Lt. Harbinger seems to have pulled himself up by his own bootstraps. Unfortunately, I think it's obvious Mr. Lewis is operating under a delusion. Which might break under all the stress the participants in the program will experience."

This was something Gabriella found hard to imagine Sean Lewis doing. No matter how much she disagreed with the beliefs of her star applicant. "Has something come up previous to this? Can I ask what the background check produced?" She didn't believe it could be much different from the one she always conducted with an applicant. And that came before any recommendation to enter the interview process was assigned.

Dr. Adversier stood up and answered Gabriella in the tone of voice which warned her not to waste too much more time on this topic. "I am sorry Ms. Messenger, but the background checks are confidential. And don't worry about the tests. I'm confident the lieutenant is the type of person we need. The tests Mr. Lewis will be taking are just additional personality tests for his file. We already know where he stands on religion. We don't want to risk lives unnecessarily. It's going to be dangerous enough."

Gabriella was a little frustrated by thinking of some of the other names she was going to recommend. "But Dr. Adversier, how can we eliminate all the first responders with religious backgrounds? Our pool of applicants will be severely limited."

Resistance on the part of his assistant was unusual. So Dr. Adversier decided to put down his rising anger and give a more detailed explanation. "But Ms. Messenger, as it turns out, we must. I have already eliminated several of your previously accepted recruits. It was strictly based on the data and results of some previous tests made of the program. You'll be pleased to know it was, in numbers, very few. I can't discuss the data in detail but let me tell you about a story I feel demonstrates the problem quite vividly."

He was now the classroom professor. "A veterinarian was called to check on a flock of sheep. They had all collapsed into unconsciousness. It turned out only one or two of the group had been chased by dogs. But, despite this fact, the whole flock was overcome by extreme fear and was near death. They were on the verge of giving birth as well so the veterinarian and shepherd had to work feverishly to try to save both the ewes and lambs."

Gabriella knew better than to interrupt the doctor

in his role as lecturer but she did it anyway. "But sir, I don't exactly understand how this applies to our applicants."

The doctor decided to be patient. "We're about to give birth to something which has not happened before. The potential power is almost unimaginable. These religionists call themselves 'sheep'. From my knowledge of them and their history it's an accurate description. The veterinarian said he didn't know how all the sheep were affected at once but he'd seen it over and over. We are moving into a future the primitive mythologies of the past never dreamed of but often try to stop. We don't have time to revive multiple volunteers. If they can be overcome by emotional hysteria they are therefore at a greater risk of injury or death. It would endanger the success of the whole program." He ended the discussion by picking up his brief case and moving toward the door. "Now if you'll excuse me, I've got another appointment. Be excited, Ms. Messenger. Our team is ready and we're going to be making history! Maybe, even re-making history."

With that Dr. Adversier walked out. Gabriella, slowly and thoughtfully, gathered her papers from the pristine desk top. Then she left the empty, uncluttered, impersonal office.

"Quantum Man stopped to Color Charge the Full

Spectrum. They had been going here and going there, following his commands. Now they were tired and even felt a little faded and dim. The Full Spectrum needed everything they could receive from Light Writer. Then they could give Light to those they would meet in the future. He set the Color Force on guard. His charge washed over and through the Full Spectrum. Their colors 'sprung forth like clear shining after rain' and they were brilliantly illuminated from within. The Color Wash allowed them to put the events of the past on the background Light Writer created. This made the larger, overall purpose Quantum Man had for their lives visible. The Spectrum was part of the Great Exchange which would lead to the Grand Reunification.

The Network could always tell when the Spectrum had been busy but hadn't stopped to fully be with Quantum Man. Their color was duller and their light was easier to quench. The Network could then use the Quenching Beam on them almost without restraint. It made individual Spectra feel disconnected or paralyzed under a heavy weight of darkness. The interesting thing was it had no real affect whatsoever on the Full Spectrum. With Light Writer occupying space in their hearts they had full transmission capacity, even if they didn't know it. The Spectrum was forever connected to Quantum Man. The Network and their Beam couldn't put out, or even diminish, the Team's lights nor occupy any space within them.

But the Beam had full effect on the Empty Lamps. It used the trauma of a dramatic reduction to the already reduced amount of light they possessed. It weakened every aspect, inside and out, of the Lamp. Their small transmission capacity lights were frozen. This allowed the Network to move right in and occupy all the empty space available.

At times, individual Full Spectrum members, or Spectra, "felt" disconnected and paralyzed. But, in reality, they couldn't be. It came from trying to run on their own energy in their own way. They just needed to go to Quantum Man to get recharged and find out what the source of their problem was. Yet, as long as they didn't, the Network was happy.

Happy but confused. The Network never understood why light sources would stumble around in the hostile darkness. All they needed was Quantum Man to restore them to full brilliance. The Network loved the dark and working in it. The dark allowed them to do what they needed to do and believe they were not observed. And they never forgot how Net Man was the source of their power. Well, they couldn't even when they wanted to. He wouldn't let them."

Wow, Peter thought, this is some story line. I hope the ending is happier than the beginning. He looked up at the clock on his wall. Maybe I'm just tired. It's later than I thought. The note on his desk reminded him of the early appointment he had scheduled for tomorrow. Clearing everything away he went to bed.

CHAPTER 4

After waking up from a restless night, Peter looked out his garden window. The rain had stopped. Drops of water had formed on the outside staircase banister. Like prism jewels they were reflecting the red, green, gold and blue of the rising morning sun. It's as if I'd put the Christmas lights back on, Peter thought. Beautiful! Unexpectedly a sparrow landed on the rung below and brushed many of the sparkling raindrops away with the shake of one tiny wing. Peter shook his head. It was sad something so beautiful should be so fragile and temporary. Well, you were just water and reflected sunshine but I'll remember you, he thought as he turned back to his work.

Total reflection of the Quenching Beam! What a shock. The ray bounced off the target as if it had struck a mirror. The Network was still in disbelief. The white light exploding into the darkness and coming right back at them felt directed. Impossible of course. Their intended victim had been lured and the Boss's Beam Spitter had been set up. So there couldn't have been any Light Incident Beam sent from the enemy to deflect the Quenching Beam. Unless, it was an inside job and a Full Spectrum spy was present! Rage filled them. The intruder's light and color still as bright as ever. Only a Full Lamp could survive the released energy of a deflecting incident. It had only happened one other time and, as before, they knew the Light couldn't be put out, overwhelmed or overcome by them. It was too dissimilar. But they could destroy the Lamp. He wouldn't have time to tell anyone. They had planned for him to be frozen and contained within a body the Network would control. Frozen Light was their favorite – just like dessert! All of the benefits of life without enough light present to crowd them out or even reveal their presence. Unfortunately, it's all or nothing with Quantum Man. And the Boss was being so careful too. He hadn't wanted any more of the Full Spectrum to be caught in this net. He still thought Quantum Man might not find out about his plan in time to stop the ultimate results. No one in the Network dared to even think he might have made a mistake. They knew it might be their last thought in this world. But the Network had made a made a glaring mistake of its own. They had been seen."

The fire in the national forest was raging. Light from the fire helped to illuminate the three people standing beside the KCBC press van. Ray Angstrom was tall, athletic, and thirtyish. He was one of the project volunteers and was finding a lot of amusement in the newly arriving fire units.

"Well, I'm so happy we were once again able to clear the way for our late arriving counter parts. How many times has it been, Gabby?" He laughingly turned to look at Gabriella Messenger and the KCBC Anchor, Angelique Tidings. They were standing closer to the van and any protection from the heat and cinders it could give them.

"This is the third event this week." Gabriella said trying not to cough.

Angelique was watching a greenish yellow band of light passing overhead. It was the Regeneration Beam. It was being broadcast from the physics laboratory at Mountain View into a Mountain View mobile unit on the ridge of the mountain. The dark part of the Beam looked constant. But it was replenishing itself nano-second after nano-second.

Ray was in a high state of elation. "This is only the beginning, Gabby. We'll be replacing those dinosaurs any day now," he said smiling cheerfully as he walked back toward the shelter of the van.

"Is that the plan, Ms. Messenger?" Angelique asked with air of mild interest.

"Gabby and Ray, please," responded Gabriella in a tone her friends would identify as guarded.

Ray seemed oblivious to the stress of the other two. "Yeah, please. When someone calls me Mr. Angstrom I start looking around for my father," he answered still jovial and smiling.

Angelique smiled back and said, "I understand completely. Feel free to call me Angelique. Thank you very much for staying around to answer my questions. If you could please come inside the van we can watch the broadcast and then I can get your response."

All three stepped into the van and felt instant relief from the heat and most of the smoke. While being a nice, large size van it felt crowded with the three of them plus a camera man, technicians and driver. But everybody was still able to see the monitors when the broadcast was re-cued and started. Burning flames and little swirling bits of smoldering embers were the background for the anchor as she gave her report.

"This is Angelique Tidings reporting from the site of the Angel Mountain Forest Fire. A fatal accident occurred today related to this fire. The victim was Lt. David Harbinger. He is one of the paramedics in the special team of first responder volunteers called Spectra Team. The Spectra Team has been involved in some of the most dangerous and spectacular emergency rescue events of this past year. The fatal accident took place in the Physics Lab at the Mountain View Institute of Technology."

A short video montage of rescue events followed where the Spectra Team was the first responder to the site. At first glance, their dark uniforms were not unlike those of the other emergency units now arriving. But the high definition cameras had picked up a surprising glimmer of light from the group. It caused Angelique and the technicians to wonder if the Team's uniforms were made of some very different material. It would have to be incredibly reflective of any available light. The interview with Spectra Team member Allen Lee was coming up next. Angelique and her co-workers planned to subtly observe Ray and Gabriella to see what their responses might be.

Allen Lee's voice was low key and, as usual, he was as confident and assured as Gabriella expected. Gabriella smiled. She knew what a wacky sense of humor lurked beneath the consummate professional's stoic "game face."

"Despite the accident we were able to get here ahead of the other response teams. We relayed the preliminary assessment of the situation to them and make a few rescues. Now, since fire and police personnel have arrived, we will be moving on to another call." Allen finished his statement and he was off. No time for questions.

Angelique wondered if her guests had noticed the glint and gleam of, not just, the paramedic's uniform but his skin as well. Her team had already analyzed the video. They found the underlying color of both skin and uniform was the same sickly green as the beam passing overhead. Looking at Ray she thought she could detect the faintest gleam and tinge of green but it might just be imagination.

Now came the most surprising part of the story she had covered tonight. Her producer had informed her of it right before the broadcast wrapped up.

"This breaking news just in. We will go to the Mountain View Physics Department for an announcement by the Director, Dr. Lumière Adversier." The scene switched to a large and cold looking college auditorium. It was a good match for the personality of the well-known professor who was approaching the podium in the center of the empty stage.

"As you know a unique team of rescue personnel has been in operation this past year. This special group of heroes have come together for a two-fold purpose.

First, is to rescue lives from situations of extreme danger here on earth. The second is more unique. They want to answer a question. Will it be possible to do emergency rescues of those who have so valiantly committed their lives to the exploration of space? Moving farther out into space and staying longer will create new logistical problems. How to deliver the personnel and supplies needed to reach and rescue those in an emergency situation is the question. It may not be physically possible through conventional means. Lt. David Harbinger was a Spectra Team member participating in this experimental pilot program. He made the ultimate commitment to the saving of lives today. This was the first, and I must say, unexpected and inexplicable fatality in a year of successful rescues. But rest assured there will be a thorough and full investigation. Thank you."

They brought Angelique immediately in to finish up the on-location broadcast. "Lt. Harbinger was serving courageously and faithfully on mankind's front line of defense. He was one of the many unknown heroes. Unknown until today. That's it for tonight."

The whole news crew turned their attention to Ray and Gabriella. Gabriella looked subdued and contained. Ray still looked exhilarated or excited, Angelique wasn't sure which. Angelique opened the conversation with, "Now, could one of you explain what happened today?"

Gabriella took a breath and said, "Not on the record. I've been here all day and don't have any first hand information."

Angelique recognized Gabriella's response was not a definite rejection. "Would you be willing to talk with me if it was off the record? We could go back outside if it would be better for you."

"Yes, I'd be happy to do that." Gabriella said and stood up to leave with Ray right behind her. The fire had moved on a little but it was still hot and smoky outside.

When they had moved a distance away from the van Gabriella stopped and opened up the dialogue. "As I said, I've been here all day as the on site observer but Ray is in the lab."

Angelique thought perhaps that would account for Ray's odd response to the events of the day. "So Ray, you were in the lab when the accident happened?"

Ray looked pleasantly at her and said, "No, I'm here now. I was called in to take Lt. Harbinger's place after the accident."

That was the oddest reaction he had shown today. It took Angelique off guard, "You..were..uh are..there?"

Ray laughed and shook his head, winking at

Gabriella, "Yes, I came in right after I got the call about Lt. Harbinger. This was his first time in the Cloud Chamber but something went wrong and he couldn't be paired up. From the description the Doc gave I'd have to say he died of heart failure after being zapped with the lightning bolt."

Gabriella shook her head in an attempt to get Ray's attention and the expression on her face was a frown.

"Lightning bolt?" Angelique asked. Ray's expression had changed to one of alert attention but Angelique had the feeling it was not for her.

"Well, we call it that because that's what it feels like. It's the Laser Regeneration Beam if you want the formal term for your story. In this case vaporization never took place. Look, I need to get going. Our time is almost up here at the lab and there is one more quadrant I need to check. Gabby is the one to ask about how this whole thing works." He waved cheerily and started moving away and toward the fire.

Gabriella, still frowning slightly, called after him, "You be careful. That's the worst part of the fire."

Smiling Ray yelled back, "Will you stop worrying. I'm not really there, remember? See you when you get back here." He hurried up the path of the fire break, passing many of the incoming firemen, and was gone.

Now Angelique was convinced the paramedic still had to be in shock from the accidental death of his team member. She expected Gabriella to confirm this when she asked, "He's not really there? And he'll see you when you get back here? Now I'm confused. Would you be willing to explain what has been going on?"

Finally, a smile broke through Gabriella's frown as she answered, "Sure. What do you know about quantum entanglement?"

Probably not enough to understand what you are going to tell me, Angelique thought. "I know Einstein called it 'spooky'."

Gabriella nodded in agreement and said, "It often lives up to its name. As Ray told you, he isn't out here at the fire. He's in the Cloud Chamber in the Physics Department at Mountain View. Here he's a carbon-crystal recreation of himself. But he not only knows he's actually there in the Cloud Chamber at school but absolutely feels the reality of being here. In fact the greenish-yellow band of light above our heads is the Regen Beam being broadcast to and from the Cloud Chamber. It's Ray, Allen and the others being regenerated over and over again so fast that neither we nor they can tell they aren't here. For all practical purposes Ray is here and there simultaneously. This process is a revolution of unlimited potential. It could allow us to send first responders from an earth-based lab to emergencies occurring anywhere on earth or in space."

These revelations were mind blowing. But Angelique decided to change the direction of her questions. "We've been told about, and have witnessed, what looked like the death of members of the team in the field. Yet we have also seen them immediately come back seemingly alive and well. It didn't happen to Lt. Harbinger. What was the difference or could this be an eventual side effect to such an extreme experience? And are there others?"

Gabriella's smile had disappeared and the sense of constraint had returned, "It's called 'Quenching'. It's when we use a 'quenching agent' such as temperature change to halt the process which is creating the Quantum Pair in the field."

Angelique asked, "Quenching Agent"?

Gabriella looked up as a plane flew over low and slow. It was delivering water siphoned up from the local lake to the fire line. "For example, if you abruptly submerge hot metal into a cold liquid its crystalline structure will be fixed. To create the Quantum Pair we try to get the temperature of the volunteer as close to absolute zero as fast as possible. To reverse the process, we bring the volunteer in the lab back to a normal temperature with equal rapidity."

Angelique was thinking how uncomfortable the heat from the fire felt even at a safe distance. "But aren't you talking about something going way beyond the limits of human tolerance? Do you think that's what killed the lieutenant?"

The heat and smoke was starting to get to Gabriella. It was a little irritating to be asked the same question again. "As I said, I wasn't there so I can't say anything about what I haven't observed for myself yet. From the little Ray told me they hadn't even got to the pairing stage yet. Also the 'quenching' happens at what is basically the speed of light. It happens so fast the volunteers have no sensation or memory of the experience."

Something Ray had said came back to Angelique. "You said it happens so fast the volunteers have no sensation or memory of it yet Ray just told us it's like being hit with a lightening bolt."

Gabriella smiled again, "Maybe he's trying to impress you. The truth of what they are doing is astonishing and amazing but the process may not sound as impressive. It happens between thoughts and is hard to describe. Look, each potential team member is given rigorous physical and psychological testing. The only physical side effect seems to be a greenish-yellow jaundice-like condition to the skin. This is easily treated with ultra-violet light. The psychological effects are one of the reasons we are doing the pilot project. These volunteers are the healthiest human beings, mentally and physically, we could find. And, so far, they seem to have no negative side effects from the quenching process."

At this point Angelique decided to ask the question she had been holding in reserve, "How about spiritually?"

"Spiritually?" Gabriella said and this time her surprise was evident.

Angelique then moved in with the series of questions she had been dying to ask. "There are now many witnesses to these 'deaths', or 'Quenchings' as you describe them. They have reported being extremely disturbed. Not just by the 'death' itself but by the reaction of the individual volunteer and the whole team. They seem to get a kick out of it. Almost "an unholy joy" as one witness called it. What do you think of that?"

Gabriella was trying to figure out where this line of questioning was coming from. "I think your witnesses may have a great deal of imagination or don't understand the situation as it's unfolding."

Angelique was starting to enjoy the hunt now. "Most of them are firemen, doctors, paramedics, even some former co-workers of the volunteers. A lot of them say the volunteers have become different since they started the program."

Gabriella was going to try to wind down this interview. "I'm not the person to ask about spiritual questions. It's not one of my areas of expertise. What I can tell you is there have been no 'deaths' in the field. Quenching is applied when the emergency personnel's Quantum Pair has finished the job. Or has been disabled while doing the it. The Regeneration Beam is stopped and the volunteer will collapse back to, or return to, his original state. That's all. No human being has been injured or killed. The real person is in the Cloud Chamber back in the lab. I'll admit it is, at times, disquieting since every atom of their mind and body has been paired. Even I feel it is the person I know. But it's my problem not theirs' or the process."

Angelique reached into her jacket pocket, pulled out a newspaper clipping and handed it to Gabriella. "Do you know this cartoon strip?"

Gabriella took it and looked at it. She felt the dawn of understanding break through but her face showed no particular expression. "Yes, I know it."

Angelique was not discouraged at all. "And the cartoonist is a friend of yours?"

A little angry yet interested in where the anchor was taking the conversation Gabriella said, "Yes. OK, what's this all about? Of course I know Peter. We've been friends for years."

Angelique had been briefed about Gabriella by the aforementioned Peter, so was happy with her reactions so far. "Have you been following the strip?"

"No." Gabriella said.

"I thought he was a friend of yours." Angelique asked.

With her friend very much in mind Gabriella said, "That cartoon is just not one of my favorites and I don't have a lot of spare time to waste."

Peter said you'd say that Angelique thought. "It's a shame you haven't been following it. The story line for the last year and a half has been eerily similar to the reports coming out about this program. For example, here he has Quantum Man giving an explanation of how he can be in more than one place at a time."

Gabriella, reading the strip out loud, agreed it was a shame. "Peter has written: 'I quote that great physicist Yogi Berra: When you come to a fork in the road - take it.' That sounds like Peter. And it's a pretty good explanation. But, are you suggesting I might be a source for this information? I don't often quote Yogi Berra."

Finally at the goal she had been heading them

toward, Angelique said, "No. I was hoping you'd find this information interesting and it would make you willing to meet with Peter, myself and our pastor."

Sounding incredulous Gabriella said, "Our pastor?"

Gabriella couldn't see the color of Angelique's cheeks in the smoke dimmed light. But Angelique could feel her face flushing with a rare blush. "I know. Most people would never assume I was a Christian. In the past, I've sometimes gone too far to prove my journalistic neutrality."

Responding with subtle sarcasm Gabriella said, "Most people would never have guessed it."

Angelique's answer had been settled some months ago. "Well, I've finished with all the pseudo-neutrality. God, and everything I am, is telling me this story is not what it seems. So I've decided to follow it until I get to the truth."

Now openly sarcastic Gabriella answered, "Impressive. But, as I don't happen to share the common delusion of Peter and yourself, I'm not getting your point."

Angelique dropped her professional demeanor and just let her heart do the talking. "My point is everything in me is saying there is something horribly wrong with this project, even evil. There are multiple reports of negative changes in the volunteers and now there's been a death."

All the arguments she and Peter had ever had came rushing back to Gabriella and she said, "This is nonsense. You don't know what you are talking ...."

Whatever Gabriella was going to say was cut off. There was a horrified scream and some loud exclamations from the first responders at the staging area and even the news crew in the van. The Regen Beam seemed to go out simultaneously with Gabriella's cell phone ringing.

Gabriella answered and said, "Ray? O.K. Yes they were. Yes, really funny. See you."

Angelique wasn't able to see the cause of the commotion. She resisted the urge to run immediately back to the van and asked, "Does Ray know what happened? Is he alright?"

After a moment, Gabriella looked at Angelique with an odd look in her face. "Yes, he wanted to ask if the witnesses were terrified when he jumped off the cliff into the fire."

Angelique was staggered. "That was a joke?"

Gabriella, looking up at the mountain of fire above them, didn't seem to hear her at first. Then she said, "Yes. Ray thought it was hilarious. I've got to pack up and get back to the school."

Angelique knew the question and answer sessions were over for tonight. There'd be no more discussions until Gabriella had thought this through for herself. The anchor took a business card from her pocket and held it out. "Here's my phone number. Please call either Peter or myself if you need to meet with us."

Gabriella didn't say anything but she did take the card. And Angelique was in total agreement. It was time to pack up and get out of here.

Quantum Man knew the Full Spectrum were not seeing themselves as he saw them. They were focused on the recent losses they had experienced at the hands of Net Man and his henchmen.

He called to them until Light Writer had their full attention. "You are like windows which have been washed clean by a storm pounding against them. The storm has passed. Now, the glow of the light within clearly shows the design of each window and their transparent, wonderful colors. Eyes will see those windows. They will desire the promise represented of light, warmth and shelter from future onslaughts. A storm of darkness has come against you but waves of the Living Light flows through and illuminates you. Be transparent and clear, living jewels shining with the treasure of the Light. Glorious Colors! You will first draw the eyes, and then the longing hearts, of those who desire to find shelter from the darkness in the Light."

The dimming, shadowy cloud of obscurity enveloping the Full Spectrum evaporated. In the fierce brightness of Quantum Man's presence they could think. They could act. They could..."

The phone rang and broke into Peter's concentration. He jumped up to get it and prayed it was the call he was expecting. After hearing the good news he went back to continue the story. It seemed like only minutes later but the ringing of the alarm clock let him know he had worked all night. "Wow, it's time to go. Good thing I set the alarm. I can't miss this meeting," he thought as he shut down the computer. "Especially not now."

Kathleen L. Daw

CHAPTER 5

Like watchmen on the wall, Quantum Man had stationed the Full Spectrum wherever it was darkest. They were his eyes, ears and voice in the silent battles of the night. They stood at their posts flashing like sunbursts through breaking dark clouds. Hidden in the net of thick darkness they listened and watched for the slightest warning of the attacks to come. Those of the darkness could neither see them nor understand what was happening. How could light, warmth and the sounds of life continue despite their best efforts.

Net Man knew something was wrong and he guessed Quantum Man was working. "Even in my own territory." The thought filled Net Man with rage. "Things keep getting way from me and I seem to be working with a broken net. Well, I'll have to see about that. I'll tighten things up around here. It's going to change or I'll know the reason why."

Terror spread through the entire Network and drove them to more extreme measures. Who knew what would happen when Net Man was trying to assign blame for failure.

Gabriella suppressed an inexplicable urge to look back and check the hallway as she opened the lab door and ushered in her guests. First in was the always prepared and professional Angelique Tidings. The casually dressed and still lanky, Peter Luz followed. They were quite impressed by their first look at the Lab of Dr. Adversier. The pride of the Mountain View campus it was huge by any standard and always filled with the latest technology. It was comprised of what had been a series of smaller labs for the use of the college's other professors. The labs and the research privileges of those professors had been swallowed up by Dr. Adversier's needs. With a stark white and clinical look it would, in most part, be familiar territory to any lab technician. The one exception would be the ten individual "Cloud Chambers" which occupied the largest part of the lab. This innovation allowed all the on duty members of the Spectra Team to be put out in the field instantaneously. However, few people were aware of that fact. The chambers were far to the back and away from the entrance behind a door. That door was hidden by the small lab office and the larger "Cloud Chamber" used for PR demonstrations. Dr. Adversier made sure any mention of how the Spectra Team worked was carefully worded. Most people would have thought the cost of running the one chamber was astronomical. Most people would not have been able to find the words to encompass the description for the expense of ten such chambers.

Most people did not include Peter and Angelique. They had both read the notes given to them by a friend on the Mountain View Board. The notes described a critical meeting about the Spectra Program. It was between the school board, the school administration and Dr. Adversier. The doctor had given an explanation, in exact terms, of the reason why the full financial details had not been revealed to the media. The costs were already covered by the generous endowments given to his research by well-known donors. And those same donors continued to make substantial gifts to other Mountain View programs. They were given in honor of Dr. Adversier being on the faculty and would be for as long as he remained at the school. The administration could not disagree. So, even after years of development, few people knew exactly how much money supported the Spectra Program. But, thanks to the same friend, Angelique and Peter were again among the few exceptions.

A nudge from Peter brought Angelique's attention back from mentally assessing the cost of the lab. She realized Gabriella was introducing her to Liora Emilio, Dr. Adversier's Lab Assistant. Liora was smiling and laughing a little. She was used to members of the press trying to see as much of the lab as they could possibly squeeze into the limited time allowed them.

"I'm happy to meet you, Ms. Tidings," she said, holding out her hand. "I enjoy your broadcasts. You are very accurate."

Angelique immediately liked the smiling, petit figure. Her warmth was in contrast to her sterile, somewhat unwelcoming work environment. "Please call me Angelique. And may I call you Liora?" Getting a smile and a nod from Liora the reporter held out a USB drive. "I just want to thank you for inviting us here and being willing to explain this unbelievable process."

"It's the statement Dr. Adversier made at the press conference." Peter explained. "We thought, if you would be willing to watch it with us, we would have a starting point for our discussion."

Liora took it and guided everyone over to her enclosed office area where they could watch the recording. It looked almost like a homey living room with its comfortable rust colored couch and chairs. "You are both more than welcome. Gabriella explained how the press conference had given rise to some questions. I am more than happy to clear up any confusion or anxiety you may have about the program. Please forgive us for not allowing the camera but we do have to keep some level of security." Plugging the drive into a computer she invited them to sit down.

All four settled in and began to watch Angelique's broadcast. "Several months ago there was a tragic accident in which a Spectra Team volunteer rescue worker was killed. Since then a number of disturbing questions have arisen about the experimental program. We heard from the Spectra Project leader and Director of the Mountain View Physics Department today. Dr. Lumière Adversier has just finished a news conference he hopes will answer the ever rising voices of concern."

A close-up of Dr. Adversier at a podium in the school's auditorium filled the newsroom screen behind Angelique. In a reassuring tone he said, "I must again remind you no human beings have been killed in the field by this process. The quantum physics based process we use is like making a multi-dimensional printer copy of a human original. It's accomplished through a high speed interaction of light, water and carbon atoms. The copy has no life of its own. It is merely an animated identical duplicate of the original which can be rapidly sent to safely work in high risk situations. This is similar to the use we make of robotic arms when working with dangerous or radioactive substances. The condensate which is formed will duplicate every atom of the volunteer as it is beamed into the emergency area. We are the sum of our atoms you might say. Every facet of the volunteer makes the critical transition from one state to another. A spontaneously formed crystal-carbon fullerene cage houses the duplicate. So the condensate naturally includes a copy of the volunteer's personality. It will look and act as the volunteer would but it is not the person. At the end of the emergency event, the atoms of the copy are completely dispersed. Now concerning the tragic loss of Lt. Harbinger. The autopsy found large amounts of epinephrine had flooded his body back at the lab. This hormone is commonly called adrenaline and is triggered by the 'fight or flight' mechanism. We thoroughly test each applicant for such susceptibilies. But the medical report would seem to indicate Lt. Harbinger was overcome by extreme panic. We believe this prevented the Quantum Pairing from taking place and caused the lieutenant's heart to fail."

The program continued back at the studio with Angelique giving the tag ending. "If you understand this amazing explanation, please give our station a call as soon as possible. Well, that's it for tonight." The screen went blank and Gabriella pulled out the USB.

Angelique was the first to speak. "You can imagine the response we got. A large part of our audience called in and asked us to please give simpler explanations of what Dr. Adversier just stated."

Peter followed up. "If you could just start at the beginning and give us a run through on how the contraption works, it would be greatly appreciated."

Liora laughed and nodded in the affirmative. "Contraption is the right word. I sometimes marvel at how it works myself so explaining it again is a good refresher course."

Gabriella, in total agreement said, "Even I'd like to hear it again. So go ahead Liora."

Liora had pulled up a file and "the contraption" was already on the screen. "This is a power point presentation I take when we present the concept to schools around the area. We could watch those slides if you wouldn't be offended?" she asked.

Peter made himself more comfortable in his chair. "Speaking for myself, I feel it would be just the right level."

Angelique smiled and sat back in her seat saying, "Sounds perfect. Go ahead. And as simple as possible if you please."

Liora started with a short introduction. "I know you've heard Dr. Adversier say we are planning trips into space beyond our ability to pack enough supplies for the crews. A viable tool for replacement objects and even food has been 3-D printing. Also 3-D medical bio-printers for replacement organs, limbs etc. However, if an event completely incapacitates the crew, how do we get rescue and medical personnel to them?

With a quick click a simple animation of a piston style engine dated 1818 appeared on the screen. Liora continued her explanation by saying, "You might be especially interested in this Peter. The foundational concept for the 'contraption' is the Stirling engine. Robert Stirling was a Christian minister who lived in Scotland in 1816. He developed the concept of the Stirling Cycle and designed a simple yet unbelievably effective engine."

Gabriella gave credit where credit was due. "Yes, so effective it's been in use since the 1800s and under development at some major companies for decades. NASA also uses it in various aspects of the space program."

Liora stood up and pointed at the diagram. "In the original idea you have two chambers, one hot and one cold with a 'working fluid' of some kind, usually helium or hydrogen. In the middle of both chambers is the 'regenerator matrix.' "

Angelique, who had been taking notes, glanced at

Peter, guessing at his response.

"The Matrix?" Peter happily looked at Gabriella and said, "We always knew it wasn't just fiction."

Liora nodded with appreciation, "This is where I always get a big reaction. As you can see, in the case of the Stirling Engine, the regenerator matrix is a heat exchanger. Thermal energy is converted into mechanical energy through the differences in temperature and pressure in the two chambers. This causes the 'working fluid' to move back and forth through the regenerator. In our case, it's not the difference in the two chambers but in the atoms of the 'working fluid' itself. In the Cloud Chamber we create an optical lattice with a trap through the use of multiple laser beams. The atoms become an inert 'super fluid'. After losing all resistance to current flow, it moves back and forth through the 'regenerator beam' of light. Of course the 'working fluid' in this instance is a volunteer who is not physically sent anywhere. The volunteer's atoms are suspended within a cold, inert hydrogen Bose-Einstein Condensate. It exists in the Cloud Chamber here and the emergency sites simultaneously."

Angelique asked, "Could you explain what a condensate is?"

Liora went on to another slide. "If you can lower

the temperature of some gases to as close to absolute zero as possible their atoms will become inert and even change form. They can lengthen into a lattice or network of overlapping atoms. Ultimately, each atom reacts as if it is everywhere the other atoms are while not moving from its own physical location in the network. They become a kind of composite 'Super Atom' you might say. Hydrogen atoms are one of the best for this type of use. The human body is 87% hydrogen and we saturate the Cloud Chamber with water vapor for the suspension phase."

Peter was shaking his head and said, "But there is solid, walking, talking human being at the site-not just a vapor."

Liora brought up the next slide. This looked like a schematic diagram of a complex but orderly system. "When Darwin developed his theories he thought a cell was a simple organism. A cell was described as a nucleus with a homogeneous or uniform, jelly-like protoplasm surrounded by a wall. But we now know it's a complex system or network of metabolic pathways between many different parts or elements."

Seeing Peter's smile, Gabriella said, "Don't get too excited now. It doesn't necessarily mean what you think it means."

Peter was smiling with even greater satisfaction.

"Hey Gabby, don't interrupt this very illuminating explanation."

Angelique decided to intervene, "Don't let them distract you Liora. Just ignore them."

Liora smiled and, used to this kind of interaction with two of her three siblings, continued on. "Almost every cell in our body contains the DNA unique to each of us. When our cells need to create a new cell or duplicate, they use their own DNA as the blueprint. All the commands which formed us in the first place are still there. Just to recap, the volunteer becomes the blue print for an identical Quantum Pair at the emergency site. Those instructions are activated during the beam transmission. The condensate is housed in a carbon, or fullerene, cage that spontaneously forms at the site. Fullerene cages are made out of the carbon atoms like those found in the volunteer's own body. Every cell in our body, and even our blood, has carbon atoms in it. The cage is almost indestructible. Even a direct hit from a laser might not harm it. It is identical in all respects to the volunteer's own body. So, for the condensate and the volunteer, here is there and there is here. I know it seems human but, as Dr. Adversier explained, it's just an expendable copy."

Gabriella added, "It's as if the volunteer is in a space suit made of crystal and carbon which is an identical physical copy. The personality attributes are individually paired with a corresponding quantum dot or artificial atom within the condensate at the site."

This was definitely news to Angelique. Finishing her last entry she said, "I have never heard of quantum dots. They're like atoms?"

Gabriella responded, "Yes but much easier to work with. You may have heard them called qubits. This is the actual fulfillment of the hope that qubits could be used for the storage of vast amounts of information."

Peter was the first with his question. "But how is it possible? I mean to separate, suspend and match the atoms of the volunteers with these quantum dots or qubits without killing them?

Liora put up another slide and answered. "As I've said, in part it's because the human body is so well designed, even down to the cellular level. So we have vast amounts of detailed, organized information which is perfect for the qubits to store. In addition, Bose-Einstein Condensates may be chaotic and dynamic. The qubits can control the dynamics of the BEC, moving it from chaotic to integratable states and back again. We also achieve the Triple-Point Phase. That's the combination of a particular temperature and pressure at which the solid, liquid and vapor phases of a substance exist in contact and in equilibrium with one another. A common example we're all familiar with is water in its ice, liquid water and water vapor state. Three different phases yet it's all equally water and equally present."

Gabriella added to the explanation, "Another good example is light. We see the light when light energy generates light waves. An unseen energy is generating a phenomenon of motion seen and experienced by the senses. And for us to see light the whole phenomenon has to be made up of all three of these components. Earth is sailing through solar winds which we do not see or feel with our natural senses. We have taken those winds and generated the temperature and motion we need. Uncontrolled, the force of those winds can tear atoms apart. Controlled, they generate enormous amounts of heat and power. These are needed to create the suspension, the fullerene cage and the power to send the wave length to the emergency site."

Liora turned to Peter and said, "The whole physical universe is a trinity as you might say, Peter. All space, all time and all matter, each distinct yet passing into, through or affecting every part of the other. Light is the transformation, transportation and communication system we use. The whole process is done at the speed of light, so for the volunteers and us, it's as if it takes no time whatsoever. It's almost as if the volunteers go into suspended animation. Except they remain conscious and able to act through their Quantum Counterpart. Once the pairing takes place it's as if they are one person with simultaneous thoughts and actions. The reaction of Quantum Pairs is actually faster than the speed of light since they respond as if no distance separates them at all. Not even a separate identity."

Angelique sat for a moment and then asked, "Is that the "spooky" part?"

Liora was a little taken aback for a second and then said, "Oh, Einstein right? Well, Quantum Pairs respond as one no matter how far apart they are. You will often hear scientists talking about a simple condensate they've formed as if it's a living thing."

Angelique and Peter gave each other a quick look. "As if it's alive?" Angelique was the first to ask.

Liora put the computer in sleep mode and answered. "Yes. Some scientists have described the individual atoms of the condensate as 'thinking' they are everywhere the others are. One also said you could only 'kill it' with a laser beam of light. I can't really argue with them. I sometimes have the same feeling myself. The fact is a lot of what we've done has been accomplished through the various aspects of light. We quench the condensate through the withdrawal of light."

Angelique still had more questions. "I notice the visual light of the Regeneration Beam is always a sort of sickly greenish yellow with the dark band in the center. Why is that?" she asked.

"It's both an indication of the state of the particles and waves and the energy source acting upon them. The particles are in a superposition state. Which is two different states simultaneously, in which their spin is both up and down. This means they can carry enormous amounts of information. We move them by laser pulses. The color of the wave and particles indicates our light source. It is as unique to its source as a human fingerprint is." Liora answered with a quick glance at a clock on her desk.

Gabriella was able to add some information. "Yes. When the solar winds hit our atmosphere the particles and molecules of its white light are forced apart. You see the Aurora Borealis when those particles and molecules are recombining back into white light. That full-spectrum light show is the sun's fingerprint."

Liora gave Gabriella a quick look and said, "Say, Gabby, you just reminded me. I need to talk to you about something before you leave."

Angelique was thinking, I'd love to know what that was, but only said, "Can I ask a few more questions? We've noticed the greenish tinge to the skin and even clothing of the Spectra Team Members. Does this Super-Atom Condensate sense of being in two places simultaneously affect the human volunteer in any other ways?"

Liora was a little hesitant in answering. "Do you mean have our volunteers been feeling or acting as if they were some type of Superman or Super Hero?"

Glad they were on the same page, Angelique tried for a few more details. "Yes. Maybe as if they were indestructible or super human in some way?" she asked.

Liora wasn't quite ready to say everything she thought but perhaps a subtle hint would do. "You're speaking about Ray's joke. I asked Dr. Adversier and he says no. He said all their test results are still comparable to those they took before coming into the program. He feels it's just high spirits. I asked the project doctor the same question and got the same answer. The whole on-call medical staff has taken the Cloud Chamber trip. They wanted to make themselves the guinea pigs and test it out before okaying anybody else. In fact," she said looking at the clock again, "if you'd like to ask the doctor he's due here any time now."

At that Peter stood up and moved toward the office door. "Thanks Liora but, you know, Angelique and I have to get going. We'll see you later Gabby."

Gabriella was still reacting with surprise when Angelique immediately joined Peter. "Yes and thank you both for this fascinating tour. It was informative."

Even though she was now really curious as to why they didn't want to take this opportunity to see Dr. Adversier, Gabriella simply replied, "O.K. guys, I'll meet you at 2:00 p.m."

After returning from escorting them out she asked Liora, "Was it the accident you wanted to speak with me about?"

Liora was waking the computer up and putting in another USB drive. When she finished she said, "Yes. And the Full Spectrum."

Gabriella smiled at that. "The Full Spectrum? You haven't been reading Peter's comic have you?"

Liora was busy looking for another file and said, "Well, yes. But this isn't about that-maybe."

Gabriella sat down again in one of the comfortable stuffed chairs. "You're starting to worry me. But go on."

Liora sat down with the remote control in her hand. "When the Cloud Chamber goes into normal operation, the light band is formed and sent though the Regenerator Matrix Beam to the on-site receiver. It constantly re-creates the volunteer until Quenching occurs."

Gabriella nodded her head affirmatively. "So you're telling me there was something abnormal about the operation when Lt. Harbinger died."

Liora looked stressed and Gabriella was sure the news could not be good. The lab assistant said, "Please let me show you this video. It's from one of the older security cameras already here before the remodeling took place. I'm possibly the only person who knows where it's located and where the feed goes."

Gabriella was trying to digest this cryptic remark when Liora started the video. The quality of the recording was way beyond any security camera footage she had previously seen. The camera had a great view of the Cloud Chamber and the area around it. Liora and Dr. Adversier were there with Lt. Harbinger. The lieutenant looked his usual confident and determined self. Dr. Adversier was obviously giving him some instructions just before he stepped into the chamber. As Dr. Adversier turned away and moved to join Liora at the Chamber controls the pleasant expression on the lieutenant's face disappeared. Gabriella had seen the sharp and alert look coming over the lieutenant's face before. She wouldn't have wanted it turned on herself. The lieutenant went in and stood in the middle of the chamber. Liora and the doctor made a few decisive movements and the lieutenant was enveloped in a glowing, white cloud. Simultaneously, it was as if a rainbow had exploding into the chamber. Inside the cloud the lieutenant was still visible. He was surrounded by a full range of colors but it also looked as if he was completely lit up from within by the same white light as the cloud. In the chamber the look on his face was more like exultation than fear. Liora and the doctor stopped trying to pair him and got him out of the chamber. Emerging, he looked exhausted, like a marathon runner who had sweat blood to get to the finish line but also joyful because he had made it. At first they were supporting him but he immediately regained strength and stood on up his own. And then he looked angry. He turned to Dr. Adversier, and said something. Liora took one look at the lieutenant, spoke to the doctor and then turned as if to go. But she stopped. Stepping into the picture, as if on command, was Ray, the on-duty doctor and the rest of the Spectra Team. Gabriella could see Dr. Adversier say something. Ray immediately stepped forward, took Liora's arm and moved them both out of the camera's range. Then what she saw pulled her out of her seat. The lieutenant was now surrounded by his co-workers. The body language being expressed by those around him had a predatory feel about it. Dr. Adversier drew the lieutenant's attention with a comment or two. Then the paramedics closest to him attacked him and pushed him to the ground. They held him there while the on-duty doctor plunged a syringe full of something into his arm. Harbinger was able to push them off and get up. He called out to all of them before swaying and then falling to his knees while still fighting to stay upright. Gabriella tried to see if there was any reaction in the faces of those around the lieutenant. There didn't seem to be any response at all in the faces of those she had helped recruit and thought she knew well. Adversier spoke again and they all reacted in unison. Immediately grabbing hold of Harbinger they forced him toward the entrance of the lab and out of camera range.

Gabriella sat back in her chair and closed her eyes for a second. Looking at Liora, seeing the same tears in her eyes as she felt in her own, she asked, "Can you explain what we saw happen?"

Liora had a little trouble finding her voice. She had seen the video several times and each time it became harder to watch. "You were explaining about the Aurora Borealis and called it a full-spectrum light show. It was then that I had a thought about what might have initially gone on. We started the process but, at exact moment, there was sudden overwhelming sense of power present. I thought the pairing had failed and every molecule he had must have been scattered. Yet I could still see him."

Gabriella only nodded, thinking of what she had just seen.

Understanding how she felt, Liora continued. "The name of the Cloud Chamber notwithstanding, it really is saturated with water vapor which will not interfere with the lasers. For the transfer to work every atom in the lieutenant's body had to bond with his quantum counterpart. The light band should have formed on a straight line and he would have existed here and at the other site simultaneously. But it's as if he was already bonded in another Quantum Pairing. Instead of a suspension in water vapor we saw a bright, white cloud solution where the light was just bouncing back and forth all over the place. He was totally surrounded by a rainbow effect. He was completely illuminated with hot white light within and yet not destroyed. I just realized what we saw may have been his molecules and particles being constantly recombined."

She had Gabriella's full attention now. "But through what agency? In Dr. Adversier's press conference he announced it was the result of the epinephrine in Lt. Harbinger's body. I couldn't bring myself to buy the panic angle. But if there was epinephrine present in an amount overwhelming enough to kill him might there have been other unforeseen physical effects?"

Encouraged to hear an element of doubt about Dr.

Adversier's public explanation of the tragedy, Liora went on. "There may be another explanation. You know qubits have only two possible states. If you try to measure a quantum dot to find out where it is it will collapse into one of those two states. The quantum algorithm we use is supposed to insure any direction leading to a wrong answer or measurement will be canceled out. The direction of the right solution will be constantly reinforced. But it was as if he was constantly being reinforced for another direction. This kept collapsing the Emergency Site pairing. I've watched the recording over and over. Each time I'm struck how he looks like an athlete feeling the joy of being in the zone or...ah...a worshipper."

Gabriella looked at Liora as if she had entered into a zone, the Twilight Zone. "A what! How did worship get into this?"

Knowing Gabriella, Liora had expected a negative reaction at first but she prayed Gabby would hear her out. "I think that's only a small hint of what this project has revealed. When the doctor and I ran over and got the lieutenant out of the chamber, he was angry. He told Dr. Adversier what was he was doing was evil and the Lord was going to stop him."

"The Lord? Where on earth did that come from? All these volunteers have been tested to eliminate anyone with a religious affiliation." Gabriella was incredulous.

Liora saw Gabriella's disbelief but knew she also still had her attention. Recalling the cold tone of Dr. Adversier's voice Liora said, "That was Dr. Adversier's first reaction. He said: 'Where did this religious hysteria come from?' I was going to call the project doctor and 911 but he told me to get Ray in the chamber and the other paramedics would take care of Lt. Harbinger."

Gabriella was frowning and asked, "Adversier wouldn't let you call 911?"

Liora gestured toward the now empty screen. "As you could see it seemed unnecessary. When I looked around Ray, the on-duty doctor and all the other Spectra Team paramedics were already here."

Knowing standing procedures for the lab Gabriella asked, "Wasn't it unusual to order them all to be on stand-by at the lab?"

Liora shook her head and said, "There was no special order given for the day. They weren't supposed to be there. The call for the fire had not come in yet. So, as usual, only Dr. Adversier, the volunteer on-site controller for any new event and myself were to be at the lab. The lieutenant would have been the controller for any calls that day. He'd be sent in first to survey the size of the emergency and decide whether or not it was worth the commitment of project personnel. The project's doctor was still in his office when we received the request from the Mountain View Mobile Unit. The lab staff started getting the lieutenant ready. The doctor wouldn't be called in unless something went wrong."

Gabriella asked, "Then who called them in? Dr. Adversier?"

Liora pulled out the USB. "It happened too fast. There would have been no way for any one to call all of them and get them all here at the same time. But they were needed. They helped subdue Lt. Harbinger, get him sedated and off to the hospital."

Remembering what she had seen Gabriella asked, "You're sure?"

Liora remembered it too. "Unfortunately, I assumed it." Her large eyes looked at Gabriella and then looked down at the USB in her hand. "My attention was immediately taken up by getting Ray to work."

So he was left facing his enemies alone Gabriella thought and then caught herself up. Wait a minute, these were his team mates. They'd been there over and over for each other. Why would I even think that? But right on the heels of the thought she remembered what her first reaction had been to seeing the lieutenant. It felt as if he was surrounded by something like a...wolf pack.

Gabriella looked at her watch and it was getting close to 2:00 p.m. She said, "Just one more question, Liora, and then I have to run. In a year all the other volunteers have gone on multiple assignments but this was to be Lt. Harbinger's first one. Do you have any idea why?"

Liora knew exactly. "It was Dr. Adversier's decision. The lieutenant's name would come up for pairing and then Dr. Adversier would replace him with one of the others. I asked him what the problem was and he told me 'better to be safe than sorry'. I guess he was right but not for the reason he stated at the press conference."

Of that one thing Gabriella was sure. "No, the man I recruited had no fear."

Liora was equally positive. "Yes, I can guarantee you, Gabby, nothing had changed. Whatever killed him, it wasn't fear. There was no sense of fear whatsoever. Well not in Lt. Harbinger."

Running all the names and faces of the Spectra Team through her head Gabriella said, "What do you mean?"

Liora made a decision. "It was weird Gabby. It was as if the cloud of bright, white light around him had spread throughout the lab. I felt nothing but peace and comfort even when we were getting him out of the chamber. I was sure he'd be all right. But, as I hope you could see on the video, Dr. Adversier, the team and the team doctor all seemed extremely agitated to me. And it was all under this cold-blooded bravado they'd developed recently."

Gabriella agreed and said, "Yes, I've seen it. But it sounds as if you think there is something else?"

Liora felt a great sense of relief. She was finally going to be able to talk about what had been bothering her for months. "I'd gotten to know Ray pretty well before he was sent out on the first emergency mission. He wasn't afraid of much except insects and bugs. He couldn't stand them. Shortly after he returned I found him playing with a real tarantula. He was trying to scare the other guys with it."

Gabriella visualized playing with a tarantula. "Well, I'm not crazy about practical jokes-especially with large spiders. But wasn't it a positive change? It sounds as if he's not afraid of handling them."

Internally, Liora said another quick prayer. "Perhaps. He was laughing at how some of the guys were trying to get out of its way. I came up behind him so he was not expecting my tap on his shoulder. When he turned around, just for a second, I thought there was terror in his eyes."

Gabriella was beginning to wonder if she knew this team at all. "Terror? Liora, that's a bit strong isn't it? Are you sure you weren't reading something into a situation which wasn't there."

Gabby's reaction wasn't as bad as expected so Liora continued. "At first I thought it must have been my imagination. But as each one has come back from their first mission, I know there's a difference I can't identify specifically. They play these tricks on one another and seem to get a big kick out of it. The only ones showing outward signs of irritation, anger or of being startled are the ones who haven't been sent out yet. Like David Harbinger."

Gabriella couldn't disagree on that point. "I've noticed some changes too but nothing of the magnitude you're describing. So Lt. Harbinger didn't like it?"

Liora thought of the numerous times the lieutenant had tried to rein in some of their more extreme antics. "Yes, he thought they were taking it to dangerous lengths. He felt the team's unity was being impaired. He was concerned that eventually someone would be seriously injured."

Wishing Lt. Harbinger had let her know about this Gabriella said, "What was their response?"

Many heated confrontations flashed into Liora's memory. "I won't tell you what they called him. But I started to feel that all this bravado they've developed is like a dam holding back a torrent of fear which is about to overwhelm them. Or maybe it already has and they are just faking it. In fact, the impression I had about them and Dr. Adversier during the emergency was that they were in a state of absolute, manic horror. It was as if whatever went on in the Cloud Chamber, and the lieutenant's reaction, illuminated their true state of mind. You saw the clear shining of the light we saw on this video. Compare it with the pestilential green glow which fills the chamber and the volunteers when bonding successfully takes place. And it doesn't go away no matter how much we treat them with ultraviolet light."

Gabriella only half heard the last part of what Liora was saying. She was looking at her watch and realized she had to get going. But she had one more thought. "For a surveillance camera video your recording is high quality. Can I assume you have documented proof of other incidents?"

With a somewhat guilty smile for the "improvements" she had made to the old security feed, Liora handed Gabriella a USB. "Look, the doctor is going to be here any minute and I have to get some records for him. See me when you get back from your meeting and I'll give you everything I have."

Gabriella expected to be impressed. They both left the lab together and Gabriella found herself looking up and down the hallway again as Liora locked the door.

Quantum Man decided to send an RGB Team on an Alpha Mission and hold the rest of the Spectrum in reserve. Together, they would illuminate the situation nicely and could take any strong, direct action necessary. Other parts of the Spectrum were already in place, or getting there, and it wasn't time to reveal them yet. Many weren't happy about being surrounded and contained by the Network. It felt like they were bouncing off walls. But Quantum Man knew the wait was increasing their intensity. It would allow him to focus them like a laser at the appropriate target. He didn't want them distracted and wasting their energies. Wasted energy is wasted light and he never wanted their light wasted."

Kathleen L. Daw

CHAPTER 6

Peter and Angelique arrived at Peter's home earlier than everyone else. Angelique volunteered to see if she could find some food or snacks for the upcoming meeting. Peter felt he had to get back to work on the current Quantum Man story line.

The search for supplies being successful. Angelique poked her head out of the kitchen and asked, "Peter, did you want to stop for lunch?"

Peter had a hard time pulling himself out of the story but he finally gave a vague, "No, thank you," and immediately got back to work.

Angelique smiled, shook her head and went to fix herself some lunch and coffee. Yes, definitely coffee, she thought.

Peter stopped to think. All the times he had missed it came back to his mind with an uncomfortable vividness. That's when I tried to do what You wanted me to do, Lord, without You. I pray this will not be one of those times. Especially for Gabriella's sake, Lord.

Light Writer! Like a mighty rushing wind blowing through, Light Writer entered the vision lying dormant in their hearts and illuminated it. For the Spectrum it was as if the incandescent waves of the Aurora Borealis blazed through the sky overhead. The bold, colorful words of Quantum Man and the knowledge of what they needed to do became plain and clear. Some of the Netmen had been standing right next to various Full Spectrum members when the message had lit up their hearts. Yet none of the Network even noticed it. Light Writer could speak to all as if they were one and to the one as if the individual were all. But there had been no response, no reaction, whatsoever in any of the Netmen nearby. It always amazed the Full Spectrum how the Network was so oblivious to anything Light Writer communicated. A sense of amusement swept through the Spectrum.

Light Writer checked them and told them not to underestimate their opponents. "They have poor vision, a fear of light and can't see multi-dimensionally. But they can always see the anemic colors of the victim they are looking for. The Network also easily identifies the artificial, pseudo-colored camouflage of their fellow Network members. Something," Quantum Man *reminded them, "the Full Spectrum sometimes has trouble recognizing."* Quantum Man *had one more reminder for the Full Spectrum. "Remember, the Network has a hard time seeing your true colors while you are standing still. However, once you start moving they will have an example of reality to compare to their unreality. They will see you."* The whole Full Spectrum *knew they needed to move now.*

Gabriella pulled up in front of the home Peter had only recently purchased. It had a log cabin look to it and appeared refreshingly cool in the warm afternoon sunshine. Peter had proudly described the unique look of the house which had been hand built by the previous owner. But Gabriella didn't notice. Her mind was racing. She kept seeing Lt. Harbinger surrounded and angry. There was no way she could convince herself it had been a rescue mission. And Ray had been there. He'd been there and been a witness to the death of a team member. Yet he gleefully played a stupid practical joke up on the mountain a short time later. Gabriella had known Ray previous to recruiting him for the Spectra Team. The Ray she knew had always been pretty open and honest about his feelings and reactions to whatever he had gone through in the past. And he had gone through a lot. His past had been the great motivating factor in his becoming a first responder. Gabriella couldn't imagine Ray ignoring the death of a co-worker. He'd have said something or tried to do something about the repercussions, not add to them. A movement in the back yard caught Gabriella's eye. It was Peter coming down his back stairs with a bowl in his hand. Gabriella got out of her car and went toward the back gate in the high wooden fence surrounding the yard and its several pine trees.

Peter saw Gabriella while pulling open the gate. Just as he stepped into the yard, turning with a pet bowl in his hand, Peter said, "Gabby! Come on in. I'll be with you as soon as I feed Kitty." He then called out, "Here, Kitty. Come on boy. Time to eat."

Gabriella continued to walk farther into the yard and said, "Oh, that's fine. I like ca...."

Her remark was interrupted by a monster of a dog bounding right towards her. She didn't wait to notice the wagging tale or the open mouth smile of what Peter knew was a truly gentle giant. Gabriella bounded out of the yard with equal suddenness and decided to wait for Peter at the front door.

Peter gave the excited Kitty his meal then re-entered the house and went to let Gabriella in the front door. "Sorry about that Gabby. Come on in."

Gabriella smiled and brushed off the few pine twigs she had picked up sliding through the gate. "That's O.K. I was just expecting something a little smaller-like a cat!"

A sudden laugh came from the house and both Peter and Gabriella turned to see Angelique emerging from a room off the entry hall. "Glad you decided to come. I think it's about time we compared notes and got to the bottom of this mystery."

Gabriella was in total agreement and followed Peter and Angelique back into the room. It was all done in a honey stained natural wood which had a warm and homey feeling. There was a fireplace on one side and a flat screen TV on the other. There was a computer and an artist's drawing table near the window looking out on the large backyard. Peter's drawings and pens cluttered the table.

Peter said, "I'll get you some coffee. Have a look around."

Gabriella walked over to the window. Apparently Kitty had already finished his meal and was now playfully dashing through the yard. She watched him chase a few birds, shake a favored toy back and forth for a minute or so and then lie down with it in the shade.

Angelique sat down on the sofa which also had a good view of the window. "He's a good dog. He loves people," she said.

Gabriella joined her on the sofa. "Oh, I know he probably is. Only I had been expecting a cat after hearing the name. He just took me by surprise and, with a dog that size, I decided to err on the side of caution."

Angelique smiled broadly and said, "Well, I think I beat your time through the gate when I first arrived. As for surprises, get prepared. You're about to have another one. My pastor is here." She stood up to greet her pastor as he was just entering the doorway. It was Sean Lewis.

"You! Were you a paramedic or pastor when you applied for the Team?" Gabriella said, equally surprised and frustrated. It seemed her background checks had not been as thorough as she thought.

Sean had traded his former somewhat gothic look for business casual. "Being a paramedic was how I put myself through school. I held on to it for a while since I love it and a church can always use some extra money. But I answer to pastor most of the time these days."

Peter came in with coffee, sugar, creamer and cups on a tray. He put it down, looked at everyone with a pleased look and sat down to enjoy the conversation.

"I owe you one Peter. No two." Gabriella said, remembering "Kitty." Then she turned her attention to Sean. "So when you applied for the position in the Spectra Program it wasn't in your professional capacity?"

Sean shook his head, also enjoying the interplay between the two friends. "No, it was. I wanted to check it out. I also had prayed about it and felt the Lord was telling me it was an important opportunity. But not, I discovered, as a paramedic. The Lord has pretty much made it clear to me I'm done with that part of my life."

With another look at Peter Gabriella sighed and said, "So you prayed and God sent you on a job interview for a job you wouldn't get?"

Sean took the cup of coffee Peter was offering him. It smelled great and tasted better. It gave him time to ask the Lord for the help he knew he was going to need to get through to Gabriella. "Sure, but the real opportunity was the chance to meet David Harbinger and talk with him while we waited for the interview."

Gabriella laughed. "Knowing Lt. Harbinger, it must have been a pretty short conversation if you mentioned God. His tests showed a high indifference to anything religious."

Then they all laughed. "You're not kidding," Sean said. "When he found out what my secret identity was he was so indifferent I thought the conversation was over. But he warmed up again when we started talking shop. He'd worked with many of the same guys I had. It turned out to be the critical part of the conversation." Sean could feel Angelique and Peter supporting him in prayer.

Gabriella seemed interested. "In what way?" she asked finally picking up her cup of coffee.

Sean answered, "The guys David and I hung around with were into some wild and extreme stuff. So was I back then. David asked if I had kicked my habits or was I just a hypocrite like so many other 'religious' people."

Peter jumped into the conversation with, "Which was also an important opportunity the Lord had for David."

Gabriella was trying to imagine Lt. Harbinger's reaction to such an opportunity.

Sean responded. "I told him it was Jesus who had saved my life, changed me and continues to change me. He got me out of all the mess and gave me a life where I not only can continue to help people but I'm not doing stuff I'm ashamed of on the side."

Now Gabriella had no problem imagining the reaction. "I'll bet the conversation must have ended at that point," she said smiling.

Sean, recalling the famous Harbinger stare, smiled too and said, "Then? Absolutely. But he remembered me. After he'd become part of the Spectra Team he started to have questions, not just about the project, but about his own life. He called and asked if we could meet. We ended up praying together and he made Jesus Christ his Lord and Savior. He had been planning to leave the project but changed his mind. He wanted to stay to find out exactly what was wrong. That's how the three of us got to know him as well as something about the Project."

Gabriella was trying to think her way through what she'd just heard so didn't respond immediately.

Peter poured himself some coffee. "In fact, around the same time the Lord started giving me an almost identical story line for the comic strip. It was eerie, Gabby. The villain in the strip, Network Man, realizes one of his potential victims had escaped by joining Quantum Man. He feared that would alert the Full Spectrum to his evil plans. The day after the story had run my publisher called and said a Dr. Adversier was trying to contact me."

Gabriella had another sudden, odd feeling of disquiet and asked, "Contact you? Did you find out why?"

Peter guessed Gabriella was finding this unusual behavior for the anti-social doctor. "Yes. He said he loved Quantum Man and had been following it with great interest. He wondered if I'd like to be one of the first civilians to experience the once in a lifetime opportunity of wave travel."

Gabriella was incredulous. She knew the doctor's distain for both "pop culture" and non-professionals in science. "That's insane. In no way has it been proven to be totally safe and, even before Lt. Harbinger's death, some questionable effects had surfaced. The project might be shut down after the next assessment period."

Angelique knew this was what she had been waiting for and asked, "Really? Why is that?"

Gabriella looked at her audience of three and decided it was now or never, "The reason is the answer I did not give you at the fire. I have seen personality changes in the volunteers I recruited for the program. I got to know them pretty well during the recruitment process and everyone is different. The Ray Angstrom I first met wouldn't have gotten a kick out of traumatizing people by jumping off a cliff to his 'death'."

The sun had been moving since they first sat down and the room had become a little dark. Peter stood up to turn on the lights and Angelique continued to pursue her part of the questions they all wanted answered. "Have they all been affected in the same way?"

Gabriella nodded in the affirmative, "More or less. Some hide it better than others but all their personalities have taken a substantially negative turn. The only exception was Lt. Harbinger. In fact, I was shocked when Ray mentioned it was his first time in the Cloud Chamber. He had changed so much and so fast over the last few months I was sure it was the result of the Regeneration Effects. He even asked me to call him 'Dave' but habits are hard to break." This was something they all understood.

Angelique asked another question, "What are the Regeneration Effects?"

Gabriella responded. "It's my name for any changes I'd noticed in the volunteers who had gone through the Cloud Chamber. Dr. Adversier usually has me out looking for new recruits. Of course, the one question everyone asked first was what are the side effects? I used to give the standard list as it had been explained to me by Dr. Adversier. That is until I came back to the lab a few weeks after Lt. Harbinger had been recruited. Once I had seen him, I started my own list of Regeneration Effects. And so has Liora bye the way. The conversation we had after you left was about the changes she had noticed. She spends a lot more time with the Team and thinks it's worse than my observations would indicate." She still hesitated to tell them about the visual record Liora had shown him. Is it because I don't want to believe the obvious conclusion it suggested? she thought.

Sean broke into her silence with, "But the Regeneration Effects were different with David?"

Thankful for the diversion Gabriella answered, "Yes. He seemed to be peaceful and relaxed, considerate of others and wanting to be on a first name basis. It's definitely not the Lt. Harbinger I had known. Additionally, he had become concerned about the people he was working with. You know, how they were doing after each job was over. In fact, it was his concern that made me start to take notice of the changes."

Sean turned to Peter. "Peter, why don't you describe which storyline attracted Dr. Adversier's special attention."

Peter stood up and went over to his work table. He picked up what turned out to be a story board for one of his strips. "I hope by this time you won't be too surprised if I tell you it's about 'regeneration'." He handed the story board to Gabriella. "What's the definition of 'regeneration' in physics, Gabby?"

Gabriella looked closely at the comic strip before answering. "Regeneration means to restore something to its original state or properties."

Peter sat back down and said, "In one of Joshua Cross's research books I found a chapter he had spent a lot of time re-reading. He seemed especially interested in Quantum Entanglement."

Gabriella looked up, genuinely curious, and said, "What was his take on it?"

Peter prayed he would, please God, get this explanation right. "That the human race was made for quantum pairing with God. Sin broke the entanglement relationship. So we all became independent, separate and suspended in darkness. We lost our original state of being and all the properties or qualities of life meant to go with it. God the Father sent Jesus the Son to be the perfect example of what the God and Man pairing was supposed to be. Jesus lived as the God-Man to show us what God is like and what we're supposed to be like in Him. His death allows the Father to re-establish or regenerate the quantum entanglement. The blood of Jesus became the 'Super Fluid'. Thus allowing the Holy Spirit to pair us up and re-establish the God to man and man to God communication. We're part of the God-man compound, reconnected to God and to each other. We're regenerated."

Gabriella didn't say anything, just looked back at Peter's story board. Peter took the opportunity to go into the kitchen. He got more coffee and let in a forlorn Kitty. Kitty, feeling excluded and abandoned, was trying to gently scratch the back door into pieces. Gabriella found herself coming to the conclusion that Peter was a great artist. He had made the explanation of their conversation simple and clear enough in the strip so even a child would be able to understand it. Or maybe especially a child.

Sean added what he knew. "In Genesis it says we are made in His image. But, until we are illuminated with the Light of the World and regenerated, we don't see how to act or even just be. When Jesus told Mary not to touch Him after the Resurrection it was because He had not yet ascended to His Father. The Light of the World was returning to the One who had sent Him."

Angelique followed up with, "And, as He had told His disciples, if He didn't leave the Comforter or Holy Spirit couldn't come."

Gabriella seemed to ignore their arguments. She also seemed to ignore Kitty who had come in and lay, like an enormous, furry pillow at her feet. Instead she held the story board up and asked Peter, "So this is the story the doctor particularly asked about?"

Peter nodded and said, "It's part of a series. In the

series, Quantum Man explains to the Full Spectrum how they are paired with him. They are individually willing, active participants yet act as one. In Net Man's version of the world, all those he nets become an inert component in a network which is controlled by one – him. Quantum Man explains how every human being on the planet was born with the potential to be paired. But this potential starts to degenerate from the moment they are born and, if not paired, they will be netted. There are only two possible states of existence. One is to become a regenerated receiver, part of the Full Spectrum, shining the Light they've become part of into the world. The second is to be a component of a network which neither gives nor receives light. It just keeps ensnaring and absorbing more and more people. They are trapped in an expanding current of darkness and static with never ending noise as a constant companion."

Gabriella had a sudden flashback of her childhood attempt to rescue that other child from the Network Men. But she barely had time to acknowledge its presence when another memory replaced it. The image of Lt. Harbinger surrounded by the other members of the Spectra Team. A thought came into her mind and she spoke it out loud. "The Eavesdropper."

"The what?" was the reaction coming from three voices simultaneously. It brought her back to the present with the realization Kitty had put a comforting head on her leg and Peter had stopped speaking.

"Oh, I just remembered a paper I'd read," she said, not sure why it was such a vivid memory. "It talked about how closed, secure quantum systems could be opened to an eavesdropper. A harmful light beam is used to damage the crystal lattice. The stress of this damage creates a 'depletion zone'. In the zone the damaged crystal generates dark current and dark noise out of trapped low level light and the impurities the damage had introduced. The result would leave what had been a closed, secure system wide open to the eavesdropper. If done subtly and slowly enough the change might go unnoticed and unidentified by the system itself. The idea of a nano-robot sent burrowing in to the system was also suggested as a way to transfer more information out. And, additionally, to give the eavesdropper greater control over the compromised system."

"Hey, that's pretty good," Peter said. You could say the human race was meant to be a closed, secure system in a quantum entanglement with God. During the Fall we were damaged and stressed. This left us wide open to be attacked, used, abused and occupied by the "Eavesdropper," if I may use the term. The very low level of light we can perceive and live in only strengthens the dark current and the chaos of its static. Rebirth, or regeneration, takes place when the

Holy Spirit takes up residence again inside the believer. Damage is healed, impurities expelled and we are restored to being "Full-Light Receivers."

Sean followed up with, "He testifies of Jesus Christ and causes the believer to do the same. This means the individual human being has been re-bonded to God as he or she was meant to be but couldn't do on his or her own. Jesus had to make the quantum entanglement with God the Father possible by His death and Resurrection. His blood destroys the friction or resistance of sin to the pairing for the believer and makes them a receiver for the Holy Spirit. He returns to the Father, the Holy Spirit comes, and the human being is reborn or regenerated."

Gabriella shifted in her comfortable chair. It had begun to lose some of its comfort. This dislodged, but did not discourage, the faithful Kitty, who immediately returned to his post. Gabriella felt her natural resistance to the line of talk they were engaging in begin to rise. She looked at her watch while hoping to remember a previous engagement she might have forgotten.

Peter recognized the symptoms but continued to pursue the conversation. "We are made in God's image, to be His Quantum Pair. Without this taking place we are separated from God. We are sinners capable of doing great evil. Alone, we can't stop ourselves because the Life that should be in us, bonded to us, one with us, isn't there."

Angelique had an idea as she stirred the third packet of sugar into her coffee. "Gabriella, you remember the experiment we all did in science class where we took sugar and burned it. It's a compound of hydrogen, oxygen and carbon? The hydrogen and oxygen combined as water or water vapor and all we had left was the carbon."

Peter laughed and said, "And man did it stink. No one even wanted to get near it let alone taste it. And without God, we stink too."

Gabriella's defensiveness rose up and she said, "O.K. I got it. I remember the experiment. Let's skip the editorializing. What has that got to do with what is going on with the Team?"

Angelique was quick to respond. "The sweetness we want and expect in sugar depends on all three parts of the compound being present. If one is missing you don't have sugar."

Sean decided to answer the question with a question. "You've described the changes you observed in both Dave and the rest of the Team. Isn't that right?

Gabriella only nodded her agreement.

Sean accepted the acknowledgement and went on.

"O.K. Now, I've made some observations about the members of the team I have known in the past. I wanted to compare them with yours and see if they match."

Gabriella was silent so Sean continued. "I think some are missing certain distinct elements of the personality they used to have and seem less unique than they were. On the other hand, one had acquired something extra and seemed more genuine and well-defined than ever before. What do you think?"

Gabriella looked right at Sean but still didn't answer.

Peter sensed his friend was at least giving them her full attention now. "Gabby, you asked me years ago why I decided to continue Joshua's work. Just the other day, I happened to look out my window after a rain. The stair railing outside was covered with raindrops sparkling with all the colors of the rainbow. Those raindrops were simply water reflecting the sunlight but they caught my attention. And they were beautiful. In the Bible God said His people would be 'like dew from God, like summer showers' and they would defeat their enemy. His people might be only perishable drops of water to the world but, because they are bonded to Him, God can be seen through them. They can't be overcome and they will reflect His life wherever they are. That's what Joshua had and that's what I want my life to be."

A frustrated Gabriella said, "Peter, you're talking about the Bible and spiritual stuff. This is reality. This is science."

Angelique had pulled out her phone and said, "Let me look at my notes. I want to get your quote right. Gabby, didn't you say: 'We see the light when light energy generates light waves. An unseen energy is generating motion that is experienced in a phenomenon which can be seen and experienced by the senses. For us to see this light phenomenon all three components must be present.' The believer's life is the Light phenomenon where we see the Holy Spirit at work expressing God's will and life. Like Liora said, the Light you see is the fingerprint of the source. For example, what did you see in Dave and Ray? Was the source different?"

Gabriella didn't answer. Sean looked at Gabriella and the time. Then at Peter and Angelique. He knew they all sensed that it was time to quit for now.

Sean had a proposal to make and he prayed Gabriella would accept it. He knew Angelique and Peter were silently interceding as they sat there watching her. "I'd like to ask if you'd come to the church tomorrow morning around 10:00 a.m. There's some video footage we'd like you to see."

Gabriella felt like refusing but then she remembered the video Liora had shown her. "What a time we live in. I'm beginning to believe there's someone around every corner filming every minute of our lives." She laughed, her good humor restored and stood up. "Alright. I'll be there."

"Good," Sean said and helped Angelique to her feet. Waving goodbye they walked out together.

Gabriella got the directions to the church from Peter. Then she ruffled the fur of the disappointed Kitty a final time and headed out into the early evening darkness. What have I gotten myself into she thought as she got into her car? Whatever it was, Gabriella knew if she wanted to find out what was going on she'd have to stick with it to the end. So I will, she thought as she drove off.

"Put on the armor of Light! Put on the armor of Light!" Light Writer's words illuminated their hearts with incandescent intensity.

The primary Color Team of Red, Green and Blue was again being sent out. They could be trusted to maintain their full color constancy, whether in light or shadow. The three would bring a continuous wave of Quantum Man's whole Light spectrum to bear on the Network. The white light flowing from the Team indicated the presence of all possible wavelengths. United they were a constant pressure on the Net. Their presence could turn the Net away from their prey. Those whose ever dimming lights were frozen in Net Man's dark and empty vision. The RGB Team knew it could be done. The only question was would they be in time. Would they make it before those weak, flickering lights were snuffed out forever?

Peter stopped and walked outside. It was dark in the yard but when he looked up the moon and stars were still there. He walked to the highest point on the hill the house was set on and looked down at the city below. Lights were everywhere, singly and in clusters. The darkness wasn't very dark.

Kitty's cold nose nudged his hand. "Don't worry, I see you," he said, patting the soft head. "Ha, I should take my own advice, shouldn't I boy?" he said sitting in a garden chair to watch all the night lights spread out above and below. "I know. You see us, Lord."

CHAPTER 7

For many years dark, ugly fortresses had become strongholds of darkness throughout the land. And these strongholds were being systematically joined together in a Network by Net Man. Lives were entrapped in it with no way of escaping on their own. Once Net Man had made himself their captor, no individual could see the way out alone. But, with the Color Force as backup, Light Writer would use the RGB Team to send a wave of Light tunneling right through the fortress barriers. A captive who sees and recognizes the Light becomes entangled with Quantum Man. Light Writer fuses the two together as one and they explode out of that confinement like a star on fire. Quantum Man also had his own occupying force in the land and his Light Castles were everywhere. The battle plan would be discussed at the one Light Castle closest to Net Man's newest fortress.

Surrounded by the Color Force, it should be a safe place to talk."

Peter finished the story around 7:00 a.m. but didn't have time to finish the review. I've got to get going, he thought. I guess it will wait for me to get back. He was trying to remember everything he was supposed to bring as he left the house.

Gabriella was also out and about by 7:00 a.m., which was unusually early for her. She had called Liora as soon as she arrived home last night and asked if they could meet early at the lab. She figured, baring an emergency, no one would likely be there. Liora could show her the additional recordings before she was scheduled to be at the church. Gabby brought her USB and expected to add any other files Liora had for her. But, when she arrived, thoughts about "best laid plans" and all that flashed through her mind. Not only was Liora there but so was Dr. Adversier and Ray Angstrom. And, although she didn't see them, Gabriella felt sure the rest of the Team was present as well.

"Ms. Messenger, what are you doing here so early? Do we have a meeting I don't know about?" Dr. Adversier's voice was as frigidly polite as always.

"Oh no," Gabriella started to explain. "There is some busy work I wanted to get out of the way before this weekend."

"Since when do you take weekends off, Messenger?" Ray asked, smiling as usual. "Going AWOL on us?"

"Mr. Angstrom," Adversier's calm intervention cut through the paramedic's mirth like a knife. "Ms. Messenger is due greater respect than your tone would indicate."

"Oh, sorry doctor. I was only kidding. You know that Gabby, don't you?" Ray said, apologizing but with only a slight reduction in the amusement which seemed to be his "steady state" position.

"Yes, don't worry about it." Gabriella answered, not sure if Ray had been kidding or was taking a shot in the dark and coming unfortunately close to the truth. "And I'm sorry but I must get started or this busy work will take over my week let alone the weekend."

"Ah, I understand completely," Dr. Adversier agreed. "As astronomer Francis Baily said, 'a stitch in time saves nine.' He called it 'vulgar but true' so go ahead. We don't want anything getting out of control here."

After Gabriella said a quick thank you and went to her office Dr. Adversier turned to Liora. "Mr.

Angstrom and I will be leaving for the rest of the day. I would like you to...what was that!"

Liora looked up to see an expression on Adversier's face she'd never seen before. She was still trying to identify it when he unexpectedly asked, "Do you hear it? Where's it coming from?"

"Doctor, what does it sound like?" Liora asked but feeling she didn't have his full attention.

"It sounded like a scream. You didn't hear it?" he responded sharply. Seeing her bewildered look Adversier turned to Ray and saw him also negatively shaking his head. Immediately the doctor's familiar control took over, wiping any revealing expression off his face. "Please pardon me. I haven't been sleeping well the last few days and my imagination has lost some of its restraint." Giving Liora a slight bow he motioned to Ray and they both left the lab.

Watching them go Liora sighed and went to sit at her desk. In the back of the desk was a small drawer which was hidden by pencils, pens and various pieces of paper. Opening the drawer she pulled out a small envelope. In it was an even smaller, old photograph of a young woman holding a new born baby. Standing by her side with a tight hold on her skirt was a cute little boy wearing an astronaut costume. She stared at it until a couple of tears fell on the faces smiling so brightly out at her from the past. Wiping it on her lab coat she carefully put the photo back in the envelope and then the drawer. When Gabriella returned, Liora was still at her desk with her bowed head in her hands.

Coming back to the lab and seeing Liora obviously disturbed made Gabriella want to stop everything and ask what was wrong. But, beside Dr. Adversier and Ray, she still had an unsettling feeling other members of the Team were on the premises. Being behind on her busy work was true so Gabriella worked on it awhile hoping the rest would leave so she and Liora could talk. But that didn't happen. Giving up she called Liora to tell her she had an appointment but would be back later. Liora said she understood and Gabby knew she'd wait for her. So Gabriella filled a briefcase in her office with some of the leftover work, picked it up and left. Like herself, Liora seemed on edge, and Gabriella again had the same, odd sense of disquiet as she left the lab assistant alone.

Pull yourself together. All this spiritual mumbo-jumbo is getting to you, she sarcastically thought. Yet she found herself taking as complicated a route to the church as possible while often checking the rear view mirror. Looking for I don't know what, she mocked herself. The word 'Netmen' just popped into her mind. It surprised her but then she immediately laughed at herself. I'm going to be so glad to get this meeting over with, she thought as she pulled up to the church and got out with the almost empty brief case.

It was a small, white, well-cared for building on the corner of a residential neighborhood. It had not originally been built as a church. But the stained glass windows on the side walls gleamed and sparkled in the morning sun as did the white wooden cross at the front door. She pulled on the door thinking it looked locked but it was immediately opened by Peter.

"Come on in Gabby," Peter said as he motioned her in and closed the door behind them. "Did you park on the street? If you did, give me your keys and I'll re-park it for you," he said holding out his hand.

Gabriella handed over the keys and found the disquiet was back with a vengeance.

Angelique's voice called to her from a doorway on the opposite side of the sanctuary, "Gabby, you made it. Come on, I'll take you to where Sean has set up the equipment."

Gabriella walked through the small sanctuary, but she was thinking it looked bigger on the inside than it did on the outside. The ceiling was raised with beams of the same honey color as at Peter's house. It gave it a sense of both airiness and warmth. The sun streaming through the stained glass windows created a kaleidoscopic display of shifting colors on the soft white walls.

I like it, she thought, taking a few seconds to get through the doorway and follow Angelique to what was a classroom or meeting room. It had the same woodsy charm as the sanctuary. Sean waved to her and motioned to one of the chairs facing a large beautiful photographic print hanging on the opposite wall. It was of Jesus sitting on the throne surrounded by light. Gabriella left her brief case on a small table by the door and went to sit down. She noticed the light in the photograph changed colors and seemed alive as she moved her head. But her ability to study this aspect of the print was short-lived. Sean pressed a button and the print, along with the wooden panel it was on, rose up to disappear within the recess of a decorative wooden cupboard above. This revealed a large, flat screen TV. Gabriella figured it was connected to the high tech set-up Sean was busy with in the corner.

Peter came into the room just as Sean finished. He bowed and handed Gabriella her keys saying, "Milady, your car is in the parking lot behind the wall with the mural on it."

Well hidden from view, Gabriella thought. But whose?

"We don't want to take up anymore of your time than is necessary," Sean said as he sat down with the rest. "But would you allow us to give you some background information as a lead in to what we have to show you."

Gabriella smiled and said, "I'm resigned to my fate so go ahead with whatever you've got."

Sean was glad to begin. "Great. Would you be surprised to know the Cloud Chamber already existed centuries ago and its designer was God?"

Gabriella couldn't help herself. "I didn't know the Bible was a work of science fiction," she said with what she hoped was restrained sarcasm.

Sean wasn't at all perturbed. "You know truth is always stranger than fiction, Gabby. The Holy of Holies in the Tabernacle and Temple were always places where God desired to meet his people, apparently in a Cloud. In fact, initially, He was as willing to meet with them all everywhere as He had met with Moses but they were afraid and refused. Eventually, it would only be the High Priest who would come into a specifically designated and designed Holy of Holies. There was one way in and one way out. Death could be the result for any one trying alternate ways."

Gabriella felt confident she was on familiar ground and answered, "Well, that's religion for you. People are always afraid some god is going to kill them."

Sean pressed the remote he held in his hand and a video, without sound, began to run.

Peter asked, "Did you see this story which was run about a storm chaser awhile back?"

Every network had run the video repeatedly on their news programs recently so Gabriella had seen it. At first sight, there was a tornado just standing in the middle of an open field. Then the viewer became aware of a small running figure in the field. Against all logic, the figure was not running away from the tornado but towards it. The video switched to another segment. It became clear this was a man who had left the safety of a car to run toward the slowly turning cloud.

Gabriella nodded and said, "Yes. I thought he'd be a great candidate for the Spectra Team."

All four watchers couldn't take their eyes off the man. He was now a tiny, dark point of color standing right in front of the massive, twisting, reddish cloud of dirt and dust.

Peter said, "Yeah, or a modern day Moses. During the interview he had an interesting thing to say. The main reaction he'd felt while looking at the Cloud was that it was looking back at him."

Gabriella asked, with no particular tone at all, "Did you think it was God?"

Peter was not deceived by Gabriella's restrained

tone. "The Cloud in Exodus sounded as if it was at least as big and powerful as a tornado, maybe even bigger. So his reaction did make me think. What would I do if I saw something with such a presence of power? If I could see it outside the Tabernacle door, inside the Holy of Holies or leading the way I was expected to follow, day and night. Would I run up to it like Moses or be paralyzed by fear like the people?"

Gabriella felt they were starting the same old argument again. She responded with the closest thing to patience she could muster. "Like I said, isn't fearing God the underlying motivation for religion?"

Sean ignored the remark, brought up a power point file on the screen and went to the first slide. "This is what we think the High Priests wore to enter the Holy of Holies in the Temple of Jerusalem. The High Priest only went into the Holy of Holies once a year to intercede for the people's sins. He wore a breastplate having jewels in the full spectrum of colors. It meant he represented the whole nation when he came before the Lord. He was also required to have golden bells all around the bottom of his skirt. Those bells would ring without stopping as he walked around in the Holy of Holies. If they stopped ringing you were to assume he was dead and pull him out by the rope which had been attached to his ankle before he entered."

Trying to hide a smirk appearing on her face Gabriella said, "God would have killed His faithful worshipper?"

Sean turned toward her and said, "There's a scripture saying 'men's hearts will fail them for fear.' Maybe the bells on the High Priest's skirt and the rope around his ankle were there in case someone got the job who had heard of God's acts but didn't understand His ways. Someone so terrified of God showing up might be either paralyzed or killed by his own fear of death. And, as a matter of fact, as religion over took faith in the Temple, the Presence of the Lord was no longer reported to be there. They were just going through the motions but without any life and power. That's called hypocrisy."

Angelique reached over and picked up the remote control from the chair where Sean had laid it. She pressed a button and brought the storm chaser video back up.

She pointed to it and asked Gabriella, "When God delivered the people out of Egypt, they saw examples of the power used to do it. The plagues, the opening of the Red Sea and the death of Pharaoh's army. They saw His acts and they were afraid, even though it was all done for them. But Moses wasn't. Could you guess why?"

Gabriella watched the small figure running again. Right toward the dangerous, powerful and, to her, unpredictable cloud. "About Moses? No. But again, wasn't the purpose of this story to show the people they were to fear God?"

Peter smiled at the screen and said, "That storm chaser knows the ways of a tornado. He is experienced and familiar with it. He gives it the respect all such power deserves but he isn't afraid of it. Because most of us only know the acts of a tornado we would run away from one as fast as we could or hide if it was the only option left. The people were afraid to come into God's presence because they had seen His acts but Moses had a relationship with Him. He knew His ways. Moses knew the safest place to be was in the heart of God's power, like being in the eye of the storm."

Mentally thanking God for the storm chaser, Sean said, "Fear instead of faith is religion. But God doesn't want to establish religion. He wants to re-establish the relationship He had with the human race. Look, one day, Jesus took Peter, James and John up a mountain. In an instant, His face began to shine like the sun and even His clothing was just as white as the light they were seeing. Then Moses and Elijah appeared and began to speak to Jesus. Peter immediately wanted to put up three tents for Jesus, Moses and Elijah. However, even as Peter was speaking, a bright cloud came and surrounded them all. A voice came from within the cloud and said, 'This is My Son, whom I love; with Him I Am well pleased.' Peter stopped talking and hit the ground along with James and John. Because they were all terrified. They didn't move or get up until Jesus came, touched them and told them not to be afraid."

I wish someone would tell me I could get up, Gabriella was thinking to herself.

Peter was well acquainted with Gabriella's expressions and temperament. He was praying, Lord help us make this point clearly. "Peter, James and John were in God's presence on that mountain. When they first saw God's presence coming through Jesus Peter's immediate suggestion was to build tabernacles or tents for all three. It sounded very nice and religious but isn't it more likely he wanted to cover the presence of the Lord up? When the Cloud of God's presence descended and they heard His voice, their own fear terrified and paralyzed them. But God's presence didn't kill them. Why do you think that was?"

Gabriella's answer was short and not encouraging. "I couldn't say," she said, looking back toward the storm chaser standing motionless in the field.

Sean gave the answer. "They knew Jesus. They knew His ways. He had led them into things which had terrified them before and yet delivered them."

Gabriella continued to look at the screen for a few seconds, then looked at all three of the intent faces before her. "I know you feel this relates to the project and how the volunteers have changed so why don't you just spell it out. I've seen enough to at least be willing to hear what you have to say. I'm no expert on what God is or does. But the fact is Dr. Adversier has been adamant about not accepting any volunteers who are religious in any way. It seems odd to me." The sense of relaxation in the room was palpable. Gabriella could feel it and she knew her three friends felt they had passed over an important hurtle. Perhaps I have too, she thought, and then wondered what it would mean.

Angelique stood up and walked over to a shelf in the corner. She picked up a manila folder and brought it back. She placed it on the chair next to Gabriella. "In this folder are copies of my father's notes and all the news clippings which exist on the events we are going to tell you about. You can read them later if you feel the need for independent verification of what we say."

Gabriella opened the file. She casually looked at the carefully typed and organized notes along with pieces of newspaper articles. By the size of their headlines it's obvious they weren't front page stories she thought.

Sean said, "O.K., this is what we believe is

happening. None of the volunteers who make it through the process are religious, especially not Christian. The only exception in this particular group was David. We think it only happened because he became a Christian after he was accepted onto the team."

Gabriella closed the file. "And he was the only one who failed to pair up and was supposedly killed by the process."

Peter shook his head and said, "We don't believe that's true. In fact, we believe a number of volunteers, and others, have been killed by the process. But David was not one of them. Do you remember when a bizarre accident was mentioned as the cause of death for my predecessor, Joshua Cross?"

Thinking back Gabriella said, "Vaguely. Wasn't it because he was at Mountain View getting some science information for his cartoon when a lab accident happened?"

Peter still found himself hesitating to talk about this incident but he was the first one to answer. "Josh had been invited, along with others, to see the Cloud Chamber and to be given an explanation of how it worked. Most of the people taking the tour were inside the Chamber when an experimental beam of hyper-intense light discharged without warning. It vaporized most of them into some kind of carbon soot. Joshua was the only one outside the Chamber. As usual he had been distracted by some of the equipment. As bright light completely illuminated the Chamber he turned around and ran to the door. He could only see one person left alive so he rushed inside to get him out."

Gabriella found she did want to know what happened and asked, "Was he vaporized as well?"

Peter wasn't sure which part of this story was the hardest to tell. He answered, "No, he was struck by the beam when he entered the Chamber but not vaporized. The witness who saw what happened said it was as if the room was instantly filled with rainbows and a bright, white light. Joshua was very much alive then. It was only later that he reportedly died of heart failure."

Gabriella had been wondering where they had acquired all this information so she asked, "Who was the witness?"

Sean took up his part of the narrative. "It was a paramedic. He had been invited to witness this new technology which was going to revolutionize the emergency profession." He also hesitated a moment before continuing. "It was my father, Paul Lewis. He had been knocked unconscious. The last thing he remembered before it happened was turning around and seeing Joshua outside in the main lab. When he came back to consciousness Joshua was bending over him and telling him it was O.K. But he wasn't too sure about that. It looked as if they were in a rainbow. At first he thought maybe it was an optical illusion. Then Dr. Adversier had come in. Joshua immediately stood up and faced him. My father heard Joshua tell Adversier he knew what the doctor was trying to do but that God was going to stop him. My father lost consciousness again and couldn't say what happened next."

Angelique remembered her father's coverage of the event. "A press conference was held the next day. Dr. Adversier said overwhelming fear and panic experienced by Josh caused hysterical and deluded verbal outbursts. This was followed immediately with death by heart failure. Does it sound familiar?"

Gabriella vividly recalled Lt. Harbinger staggering out of the Chamber and the power of his anger toward Adversier.

Peter read her correctly. "Yeah, Gabby, does it sound as familiar and out of character for David Harbinger, as it does for those of us who knew Joshua Cross well?"

Gabriella was in total agreement on this point. Another aspect of the event crossed her mind and she asked, "But Sean, how about your father? Why did he survive?"

Sean was pleased they were moving along quickly now. "We were told the beam must have missed him somehow. And something else must have rendered him unconscious during the accident."

Impossible, Gabriella thought. "The way the Cloud Chamber was working should have meant neither one of them would have survived."

Sean nodded and said, "Exactly. And I don't think my father would have either if he hadn't stayed unconscious. When he finally left the hospital, like Josh and David, he had a deeply rooted conviction about Dr. Adversier's work. He felt it was not what it claimed to be and should be stopped. Essentially, that's why we're here talking to you today."

Gabriella's intense interest in the why and how of things had kicked in and she asked Sean, "Is your father going to be part of this meeting? I'd like to ask him a few questions."

She noticed the look Angelique and Peter gave Sean before he answered. "He was killed in a hit and run accident a few months after the incident."

Angelique hesitated for a moment and then said, "I met Sean and Peter through the accident. According to my father's notes he and his co-worker, Raf Billetdoux, had an appointment with Sean's father. That was on the day they were killed in the crash of station's news helicopter. The answers to why they had taken the copter and why it had just dropped out of the sky were never found."

"Just as the driver who had hit my father was never identified," Sean finished.

Peter filled in the details. "We believe they were all targeted for an accident of some kind. Right after it became obvious Sean's father was questioning the safety and purpose of the Project. And that he was speaking to Michael and Raf about what happened."

Angelique took on the explanation of the details surrounding the lieutenant's last communication. "David had just met with us and suggested the series of questions I should ask you the next time the Spectra Team was in the field. We didn't know he was going to die the day I planned to be in the field in order to ask you all those questions. None of us knew what was going to happen but God did."

Gabriella smiled slightly and said, "God knew? I'm no expert but I'm assuming you still aren't blaming God for these accidents?"

Peter answered her. "The people who died in the first 'accident' were individuals who, because of their backgrounds and interests, might find reasons to oppose the formation of the Spectra Team. I don't think you can believe those were accidents."

Angelique decided it was time to bring up the information they all considered the hardest for Gabriella to accept. "During the time the Team has been in operation, some odd news stories started to come in to the newsroom. Stories about people who suddenly seemed to vanish right in plain sight."

Gabriella watched as Sean brought up another recording on the screen and said, "Vanish in plain sight? You mean they were lost or kidnapped?"

Sean finished what he was doing, came back, sat down and said, "No definitely not lost."

Gabriella was now very curious as to what they trying to explain.

Peter asked, "You remember Alan Lee?"

Gabriella immediately thought of the strong, funny recruit she knew. He was 100% committed to his fellow team members and anything else he chose to do. "Yes. He was a great guy with a great record. He had a wife and two children he loved and was committed to his profession. The last time I saw him was the day Lt. Harbinger died. He quit the project before I returned from my last recruiting trip."

Peter said, "We'd like to show you another clip."

From the angle of the picture the camera must have been at the back of the booth Peter was standing in. It showed the entrance of the local Conference Center. Hanging over it was a banner stating it was hosting the Tenth Annual Education Resources Conference. It also had an unobstructed shot of the Spectra Team Information Table and Booth across the way in the main hall. Peter was was there representing Quantum Man and Alan was easily visible over at the Spectra Team table. Many other tables and booths were also set up in the main hall. They were all colorfully decorated with many items chosen to appeal to adults, youth and children. Gabriella saw Gil Sanchez, another one of the Spectra Team paramedics. It looked like he had entered the booth to relieve Alan. Alan seemed to be giving Gil a few instructions. Then he left and walked over to the Quantum Man booth and Peter.

Alan looked his usual confident self with broad smile and strong hand extended toward Peter. "You must be Peter. I've been looking forward to meeting you. My name is Alan Lee."

From the camera angle Peter's expression couldn't be seen but his voice was clearly heard. "Good to meet you Alan. What can I do for you?"

Before answering, Alan looked at the booth display and the two teenagers who had stopped to look. "My boss, Dr. Adversier, is a great admirer of your work. I noticed a lot of youth stopping by your booth so I was wondering if we could leave some of our brochures at your table. Especially since I understand some of our work and yours intersects at certain points."

Peter, having watched the video multiple times, remembered a sense of alertness had risen up within him right then. He had hoped it was not noticeable when he answered. "Well, most of the kids I'm talking to are planning to go into the arts. What is the purpose of your brochures?"

Alan handed Peter a sample and answered, "We're recruiting kids for the Project."

Gabriella could hear the surprise in Peter's voice as he answered, "Recruiting kids to do what with the Project? I thought it was at the experimental and dangerous stage."

Alan laughed and answered genially, "True and we're not recruiting them as first responders. We're looking for especially gifted and talented kids who might like to get an early start in some important related field. Like the way Dr. Adversier met your friend Gabriella Messenger."

Gabriella looked at Peter and thought, I bet that went over big.

Peter only said, "Go on."

Alan was not discouraged at all. "Is this some of your work? What does it deal with?"

Peter knew he had felt the sudden excitement of a potential opportunity opening up. "These are some of my latest comic strips. They deal with how Net Man has manipulated and trapped his victims. How he absorbs them and controls their wills as his own."

Alan stopped smiling. He asked, "Please explain what you mean by that?"

Peter was happy to explain and said, "Quantum Man freely offers to give his light to all those who freely receive him and are paired with him. Net Man lies and cheats to hide his true state of evil and his plans. He does whatever it takes to net his victims. They will then be forced to help him take Quantum Man's place whether they want to or not."

Alan, still not smiling, folded his arms and said, "What are you really saying through this cartoon?"

Peter started to feel the flow of the Holy Spirit and said, "This is the way Satan traps and destroys human beings. He intends to take them and everything they have so he can take over God's creation and His place in it. As he said in Isaiah: 'I will ascend above the heights of the clouds; I will be like the Most High.' He intends for his will to be above all others. Even God's."

Alan's expression didn't change but his arms came down and his body started to tremble. It looked as if he might be having a seizure of some kind. But yet his facial expression seemed impassive and undisturbed by what was happening to his body. Gabriella saw Peter give a quick look at the Spectra Team Booth across from them. Gil was talking to someone and not able to see what was happening.

Peter asked, "Are you all right?" and Gabriella could hear the concern in his voice.

Alan, with some effort, said, "Don't stop. Please continue."

Gabriella watched Sean and Angelique for a second. Angelique wasn't watching the screen and Sean looked as if he wished he wasn't.

Gabriella looked back as she heard Peter's voice continue on. "Our lives on earth are just like a vapor, suspended in sin and waiting to be bonded to death for eternity. We're like clouds without rain. We give a promise of carrying living water yet moving through the landscape without bringing any life or relief. In order for water vapor to become rain it has to bond with something. The death on the Cross and Resurrection of Jesus Christ created the solution in which a person can become bonded to Him for eternity. Sin has no affinity or ability to bond with Him and so can't ever again bond with the person who is One with Him through His blood."

As Peter was speaking, Alan's face changed. The sudden brightness of his expression made Gabriella realize how shadowed it had looked a second before. He took a deep breath like someone who had been suffocating but now could breathe. Then his whole body started to shutter as if with great pain. He put his hand out to the booth to steady himself.

Gabriella asked urgently, "Peter, what's going on here!"

Peter didn't answer. But on the screen Alan, barely able to speak, finally got a few words out. "Does Jesus love me?"

Gabriella was silenced by the question but the answer Peter gave the suffering paramedic came out loud and clear. "Yes! He died for you! He loves you!"

It was as if Alan's body was having its own personal earthquake but he smiled at Peter. He started to say, "Peter, tell my family. Tell the others...thank yo..." but his voice stopped when he started to glow with a bright white light.

There was an explosion of color and he was gone. Gabriella had a quick impression of Peter vaulting over the table and of a large number of the Spectra Team coming toward the booth. Then the video stopped. She directed her question to whoever would answer, "What just happened? Did you lose the picture? And where's Alan?"

Angelique was the first to answer, "Alan was one of those stories that came in to the news desk and then disappeared."

Peter responded. "Besides most of the Spectra Team which suddenly 'just happened to be there' we think there must have been several potential witnesses to this event. They were using their phones to record what happened. And there were also security cameras all over the Hall. Yet nothing turned up on the news or the internet. Our camera happened to be hidden by all the stuff we had hanging in the booth so we think no one else knew about it. If the camera had been seen we're pretty sure we couldn't have shown this video to you."

Gabriella's mind was racing, trying to put what she just saw in the context of reality.

Angelique tried to clear up the confusion Gabby was experiencing. "There were several facts Alan's story had in common with every one of the other stories. The first was the sudden flare of colors. It was like the rainbow witnesses said they saw when they witnessed a person disappearing. The second was a soot-like substance found around where he or she had been standing."

Gabriella was thinking of one of her recruits being reduced to 'a soot-like substance'.

Sean said, "Seconds before they disappeared they had been led to the Lord by either witnessing teams of Christians or with a one-on-one encounter with a Christian."

Gabriella's frustration spilled over. She stood up practically yelling, "Come on! Did that happen to any of the three of you? Did you disappear right after you became Christians?"

Sean responded calmly. "Of course not because the human body was created to be in His presence and to be filled with His presence. We are 'fearfully and wonderfully made'."

Still standing Gabriella said, "Don't give me quotes. I just saw Alan Lee, what, explode? So what's the difference?"

Peter had come over to Gabriella and, with a slight pressure on his friend's arm, persuaded her to sit down again. "When the three of us started to compare notes we found many of these incidents involved Spectra volunteers. But not all of them did."

Angelique had taken the remote and pulled up a power point slide with a list of names. She said, "Some of the others were wealthy or influential people of various ages and backgrounds. But there were two other things they all had in common. They had not been Christians and they all had met or were associated with Dr. Lumière Adversier."

Adversier was the one who gave me the news about Alan making a great career move and leaving, Gabriella thought. As she scanned the list of names she said, "Let me leap to a conclusion – they all had experienced the Cloud Chamber."

Peter pointed to the many names with an asterisk and said, "Yes and most before the official start time of the program."

Angelique followed up. "When I looked up some of the better known names it turned out they had been giving large amounts of money to the Project. Many had also used their influence to move the Project along and maybe hush up the questions which should have been asked. Some were replacements for those who died in the same 'accident' that eventually caused the deaths of Josh and Sean's father."

Logical, Gabriella thought. She said, "Then let me ask a couple of obvious questions. Why would a trip through the Cloud Chamber immediately change someone or change their mind about supporting the Project? And why haven't you involved the police?"

Sean, Peter and Angelique looked at each other and smiled ruefully. They were each remembering the countless, and fruitless, attempts they had all made to do just that.

Angelique spoke. "I'll answer your last question first. We believe the people of influence who came to the Lord and then vanished are just the tip of a massive ice berg of a story. In each instance the only witnesses from the incident willing to testify were Christians. Somehow they have all been written off as religious fanatics. Allegedly with hallucinations or delusions by triggered by their faith. We haven't been able to find the source for this conviction but it's widespread."

Sean gestured toward the screen. "As for your first question, it's pretty much the same story for all those who've gone through the Cloud Chamber. They all become avid supporters of the Project, even if it's a 180 degree turn around from their previous position. They are willing to give it their complete financial and political support and even their lives if necessary. We also know many have had extreme personality changes. Did you know Alan's wife had left him and had a restraining order issued preventing him from seeing her or the children?"

Gabriella experienced a sense of total disbelief and said, "Alan? I can't believe that. He was crazy about Mary and the kids."

Angelique was able to give a first hand account saying, "I tried to interview her. She wouldn't talk on camera but she told me she and the kids had become increasingly afraid of Alan. A change had come over him after his first trip through the Cloud Chamber. He wasn't even the same guy. She was crying the whole time and it wasn't just about his death. It was about all the devastation he had brought into their lives before he died."

To Gabriella, this news was as bad as witnessing Alan's death.

Sean said, "As you could see in the video, we know they can still hear, see and understand. They have a reaction to hearing a Christian witness of the Gospel even if they don't seem to have the power to physically take action. Some react with extreme hostility. But others, like Alan, hear, decide they want to be free from sin and death and belong to Jesus Christ. Then the Holy Spirit immediately bonds with their spirit. They fight for a few seconds to let us know the Lord has come through but their fake bodies can't hold together in the Presence of the Lord."

Gabriella grabbed for a fact which could be

scientifically verified and said, "What do you mean 'fake bodies'?"

Sean leaned forward. This was something they had hoped Gabriella could help them with. He said, "We're not sure. We believe when the Quenching occurs only a copy survives not the original physical body of the volunteer. Satan can't create life but uses it as a parasite would. So maybe the only reason the process even seems to work is its pattern and substance has to come from the unique individual God created. Even though distorted and weakened the copy may still have enough real life in it to allow the spirit and soul of the person to remain. Yet it is under the control of someone else. God has created a unique, one of a kind world where every snowflake seems to be different. Is it likely He would allow a legitimate science to exist where those made in His image could be copied like so many disposable action figures? Personally, I believe each of us is a one time only and only one at time creation. Jesus did not make multiple copies of Himself in order to save the human race. He multiplies Himself by the Holy Spirit bonding with each unique human being coming to Him through the way made by His blood."

Peter opened the portfolio by his chair, pulled out a set of storyboard panels. "This is the Quantum Man story line Dr. Adversier had such an interest in. Net Man is looking for those who've been traumatized in life and had an oddly unique reaction to it. Such as extreme hatred, extreme unforgiveness or, what we think applies here, extreme fear. It's the way he can take control of someone already in existence. He can't create his own slaves. He has to enslave someone who's already alive but hasn't bonded with Quantum Man yet."

All of them concentrated their attention on the storyline being revealed on panel after panel.

Angelique said, "Net Man is trying to take over everyone and is not succeeding because of Quantum Man and the Full Spectrum. This, of course, makes him even angrier and more destructive."

Knowing how Peter thought, or believing that she did, Gabriella said, "So Net Man is a.k.a Satan in your world. He's everywhere and in everybody. Isn't that a little paranoid?"

Peter thought Gabriella had retreated to an old line of discussion. "Satan isn't omnipotent, omniscient or omnipresent. He's not all-powerful, all-knowing or all-present. He's not God. But, like Net Man, he has his agents so you could say he's multi-present. He's trying to counterfeit the Body of Christ and its free will relationship with the Lord and each of its members. He may be able to know what's going on in more than one place at a time through those he controls through fear, or thinks he controls. They are of like spirit, subservient to him, and always looking for a place to hide out from God's presence. We think Satan's agents have found an ideal place to hide in those who have gone through the Cloud Chamber. They can use their victims to kill, steal and destroy and they can have the fun of torturing and terrorizing them from the inside out."

Well Pete, you're going to have a hard time proving it, Gabriella thought but she said, "O.K. let's just imagine you are right. But this isn't what happened to Joshua Cross, Lt. Harbinger or your father, Sean. It seems they were impervious to the process."

Sean was thankful Gabriella was still willing to talk. He said, "They didn't go through this process before Christ had transformed their lives but after. The Lord created the human body to live in His presence and with His presence. He meant for us to walk with Him in the garden before sin separated us from Him. I've experienced the sense of His presence where you couldn't stand upright and didn't want to."

Angelique nodded, smiled. "Or even being in the middle of what seemed like a swirling rainbow of Light where you and He were talking. And you never wanted the conversation to stop."

Sean had brought the video of Alan back on, fast

forwarded it to the moment when Alan disappeared and froze it there. He said, "We don't see the wind but we feel its effects and direction. Can I suggest to you, Gabby, that the rainbow explosion of light happening right after those people became born-again was them being set free from the bondage they were in. Instead, they became bonded to God and His Holy Spirit through Jesus Christ."

Gabriella forced her eyes away from the frozen screen and the image of a flash of white light literally surrounded by all the colors of the rainbow. She looked at Sean instead and asked him, "So, your father was a Christian at the time?"

Sean, remembering the father who was still the role model for so many things in his life, said, "Yes, he was. And my father was just fine after he regained consciousness. The bodies of Joshua Cross and Lt. Harbinger were taken to the hospital. There was a coroner's report and a funeral service. But we can guarantee you they were not killed by the process."

Gabriella noticed a pitcher of water in the corner along with some cups. To buy some time to think, she got up, poured herself some water and drank it as slowly as possible while her mind raced on. She finally came back to her seat. "So you're telling me a Christian who walks into the Cloud Chamber cannot be sent into suspension because they are already a

Quantum Pair with Jesus?"

Lord, help me explain this so Gabby won't reject it out of hand, was Peter's quick internal prayer. "We can only tell you what we think combined with an observation I'm perhaps uniquely qualified to make." He could tell he had Gabriella's attention so he continued. "When I look at people I see colors..."

Gabriella interrupted with, "Synesthesia. I know." How long have we known each other? Since we were four or five? After you turned your crayon into a car and zoomed it over the paper a couple of times you'd settle down and draw people in colors I never saw them in. But you'd insist people were those colors. And I think you'll admit I am fairly good at observation and research. When we got older you didn't want anyone to see you doing something so unusual. I felt you probably didn't want me to say anything about it. So I didn't."

Thinking of all the hoops he'd jumped through to hide this condition from other friends and acquaintances, Peter signed. "I'm sorry. I guess I forgot since you never mention it."

Gabriella smiled and said, "Neither did you, Peter. I figured you'd tell me officially one day."

He smiled back and said, "Well, that was another reason why I loved Joshua's work. People fulfilling their technicolor purposes in life through the Full Spectrum. Little did I realize the reason the Lord created me with synesthesia might have been just for this time. I'll tell you more later. But, in the meantime, will you take my word on how I have begun to see people in recent months I can only describe as almost colorless. Most of them have been in the news as Spectra Team members or important people associated with them."

Gabriella looked away and asked, "Was Alan one of those?"

Peter nodded and said, "Yes, I noticed it when he walked up. And all the rest of the Spectra Team I saw there were in the same condition. We think, because of the Cloud Chamber experience, those who aren't bonded with Christ prior to the process are in a physical and mental condition afterward perhaps no human being has experienced before. Their bodies are mostly destroyed by the process and what emerges from the chamber is some type of hybrid copy. What would happen to you if every cell, or even every atom of your body, transitioned to a state of being which was half alive and half artificial duplicate? And that transition happened at a speed faster than the speed of light."

Gabriella remembered Ray as she answered. "It might feel as if I was hit by a lightening bolt."

Angelique remembered too and said, "Yes. Maybe Ray was telling us the truth. At first overwhelmed and paralyzed by terror and fear of death their souls are still present but inert. Becoming inert, we believe opens the door and allows somebody else to take control. The soul seems to stay incapacitated. This unseen somebody is generating activity through the volunteer which is seen and experienced by others. But it's not God and the person becomes almost unrecognizable to those that know them."

Always looking for the weak point in any argument Gabriella asked, "But how can they respond to you and God if they are under someone else's control?"

Sean answered, "As long as life still exists there, the soul still has the right to choose the Lord."

Peter took up the discussion. "We heard Liora's description of the process and compared it with Dr. Adversier's version of the reason for David's death. The result is we believe it was the Lord's Presence in him that protected him. Just as it had been with Josh and Sean's father. He was already paired to the Lord. They were both fighting it together and they won."

Sean followed with, "The rainbow is often described as around or accompanying the Lord and His angels. It's His promise destruction will not win."

Angelique had been searching her notes. She found

what she was looking for and turned to Gabriella. "Light seems to be the common denominator in all these events. Peter showed me some notes Joshua made on 'quantum leaps'. One said, 'the state of an electron exposed to the right frequency of light can change from one of low energy to one of higher energy without apparently going through any intermediate changes. Exposure to light can excite an electron until it suddenly leaps to a more intense, totally different level of light. Or it can just as suddenly lose light and drop away from where it was.' Didn't Liora mention how the quenching process involved a sudden depleting or withdrawal of light? If the Cloud Chamber process forces some type of 'quantum leap' how might a human being be physically effected?"

How many of the systems in a human body depended on light? Gabriella asked herself. It was a moment before she could put her thoughts into words. "But all those reports about the release of multiple colors surrounding those affected and concluding in an explosion of white light. If they are accurate it would mean even the electrons of their bodies were being extremely stimulated. How could they survive?"

She moaned a little and put her head in her hands. The faces of every one of the thirty volunteers she had recruited came flooding back into her mind. Were they all lost! A soft whining sound and wet nose pushing at her brought Gabriella back to the now. Peter had often brought Kitty with him to the church. Usually the dog was content to wait for Peter near the back door so he'd be ready for a quick get-away. But this time the gentle giant seemed only concerned about Gabriella. The object of his concern absently patted the enormous, furry head lying gently on her knee.

Then Gabriella sat up straight and said, "So all this time, it was fight and not flight!"

Peter asked, "What was?"

Gabriella was still thinking it through but said, "For Josh and Lt. Harbinger. Fight, not flight was the reason for all the epinephrine in their systems. They were fighting against the process. Adversier suggested it was fear to send our expectations about the cause of death in that direction. Just like when I assumed Kitty was a cat. What does this mean for all the other recruits I brought in? Are they all dead?"

Sean hated to say this but answered with what he felt was true, "Physically? Essentially yes, but not absolutely lost yet. Their body is basically gone but there's still hope for their souls. Jesus said not to be afraid of those who kill the body but cannot kill the soul. He said rather be afraid of the one who can destroy the body and cast the soul into hell. It may feel as if they are in hell right now but the Lord still has a way of escape for them if they'll take it."

Gabriella seemed almost to be speaking to herself as she asked the next question. "But if Josh and David won the battle, why are they dead?"

Angelique was sure of her answer. "Satan couldn't destroy their souls but we believe he moved on a human agent to destroy their bodies for him. We believe it was Dr. Adversier. And we believe he was behind the hit and run death of Sean's father."

Gabriella stood up and gave Angelique a quick look full of decisive awareness. "I have something you need to see," she said as she moved over toward the briefcase she had left on the table by the door. She reached in, pulled out the USB with Liora's video and walked back to Sean. "Watch this. I believe it will verify what you believe," she said.

While Sean was busy plugging in the USB, Gabriella picked up the manila folder thinking Liora will want to see these stories. The video had already started and Sean, Angelique and Peter were focused on the activities being revealed. Gabriella finished stuffing the folder in her briefcase and turned around to look. Lt. Harbinger was already standing up and surrounded by the Spectra Team. As Gabriella saw it for the second time it dawned on her that the lieutenant was not the only one who was surrounded in the lab.

Liora! I have to get back to the lab! she thought.

The screen went to blue and the three who had been watching it sat silently for a moment. They were re-experiencing all the emotion they had first felt when they heard about the lieutenant's death. Only it was worse because now because they were witnesses to his murder.

Peter finally turned in his chair. "Gabby, does Liora..." Then he saw something that brought him to his feet yelling, "Wait, Gabby! Wait!" Peter ran for the empty doorway followed by Sean.

Angelique walked over to the table where Gabriella's open briefcase sat abandoned.

Sean came running back in to grab his car keys and Angelique. He said, "Her car is still in the lot. The professor's men might have been waiting for her. We'll take my car and pray as we go! She shouldn't face Adversier alone!"

It had only taken a few seconds for the classroom to be deserted except for Kitty who was whining and pawing at the locked back door. But the frozen Alan Lee video automatically started to run. Peter jumped over the table again and the Spectra Team started to move toward him once more. Then the video finished and started over again. The computer was the only light source in an empty and slowly darkening room. It continued to display its light show in an ever quickening tempo.

"The Team was concerned. They now had an additional member who wasn't part of the Full Spectrum: An Unfilled Lamp. Quantum Man had made it clear he wanted her for this battle. She wasn't part of the Network so she wasn't totally without color but she lacked the intensity of a Full Spectrum Member. They were Light Writer's living "light to sound" converters. They had seen wave upon wave of Light Writer's words just bounce off her light barrier. She had the necessary receptors which could receive what they were telling her and fill her with Quantum Man's Light. But they were off. She wasn't like the Network whose receptors were entirely disconnected but she was still empty of the Full Light. And they were going into battle. The Team was receiving the transfer of energy from Light Writer now along with the angle of attack. It was to be an Alpha attack, direct and straight through to Net Man. The Team turned to go but immediately realized – she's gone! What if the Network captured her? What if she created an incident and prompted Net Man to use his Beam Splitter? The attack might be totally reflected or they all could be dispersed like a vapor in an evanescent wave. Except for the Unfilled Lamp. She could become part of the Network. It was critical that they get to her first!

CHAPTER 8

Net Man noticed the change immediately. He was an expert by now in the Spectral Energy Distribution of the Full Spectrum. He could tell there was still an energy gap. The Lamp was showing luminous flux in the lack of brightness and color intensity. Quantum Man's complete radiant energy had not joined them together - yet.

Yes, not bright at all to come here alone and isolated, Net Man thought. But would she stay alone long given her condition? Would Quantum Man send a RGB Team? He could counter with an "Anti-rgb" Team from the Network. They looked just like an RGB Team to a natural observer but nobody knew better than Net Man what the difference was. Once excited and in Quantum Man's radiant flux an RGB Team had unlimited power to oppose his plans. They'd come at him from the front, back and side with Light Writer in the background. He'd have no shadows to hide in and all his illusions, deceptions and lies would be visible. He'd better snuff this Lamp as soon as possible.

Gabriella rushed through the open doorway in front of her but came to an abrupt stop. Already in the lab were Liora, Dr. Adversier, and almost all of the Spectra Team first responders and medical personnel. They were silently standing in a circle surrounding Liora. And, except for Liora, they all simultaneously looked in Gabriella's direction. But only the doctor had an expression on his face. It was one of surprise and it disappeared immediately. She felt, rather than saw, the last two team members come through the door.

Gil was one of them. "We didn't see her come in," he said as he and his partner moved to block the door. They positioned themselves within grabbing distance of Gabriella.

Dr. Adversier didn't respond to them. His face configured itself into one of his frosty smiles as he pleasantly said, "Looking for us, Gabby?"

Gabriella decided to ignore the situation and Adversier's unusual informality. She said, "Oh, there you are Liora. As I arrived on campus I heard about a new fire and I was hoping you'd come to the site with me and help set up the Mobile Unit. Is it your turn to go again Ray?" Gabriella moved toward Liora as if to take her arm but a couple of the first responders blocked her.

Liora finally reacted and yelled, "Gabby, get out!" She struggled with the Team member who had taken hold of her without warning. But the expression on her face had no fear, just anger.

Dr. Adversier turned to her. In the patient tone of a parent speaking to a misbehaving child he said, "My dear, please, don't get hysterical. I don't want another news conference where I have to make the sad announcement that my lab assistant was a victim of her own fear. No, that would look bad for the program."

Hearing the professor speak, Gabriella found she had a feeling of sick disgust sweep over her, but it gave her an idea. "If you're not feeling well, Liora, maybe I should take you home," she said trying to move closer to the imprisoned lab assistant.

Adversier's smile had disappeared but the long-suffering tone remained. "Ms. Messenger, you have this annoying compassionate streak which just flashes up out of nowhere. But it won't be a problem for long. Ray will take Liora home. l heard she just accepted a new job and has to leave immediately. You were a good assistant and I'll miss your skill but it can't be helped.

You've been much too inquisitive."

Ray moved over to where Liora was standing. Her frustration was greater than any fear she might reasonably have felt. They had caught her with all the evidence while she had hung around waiting for Gabriella. "Gabby, they caught me with the files. He also knows who you've been meeting with and what they've found out."

The doctor smiled at that. "Yes, one of my team happens to be Ms. Tidings editor. He kindly explained about the expose' being planned and promised to kill it. So I don't want you to be anxious. Anxiety is a killer where you're going you know."

"The jig is up" was the phrase that jumped into Gabriella's mind. I hope I'll have time to find out what that actually means, she thought. And then her curiosity spilled over. "How did you ever get someone like him into the Chamber?"

The professor loved to reveal just how smart and devious he was so he was delighted to explain. "For different reasons than our noble rescue workers. You know, willing to lay down their lives for others etc., etc. No, for someone like Ms. Tidings' editor it was greed, lust for power, all the usual stuff. When I was able to prove he could be in two places at the same time without anyone being the wiser, that was it.

You'd be amazed at the infinite number of reasons which can be used to convince someone to sell a soul. I'm never amazed but you would be."

Gabriella moved to sit on a chair near one of the lab tables. She was trying to find a better angle on Stan, the Team member holding Liora's arm bent behind her back. She responded, "Appalled more likely."

Dr. Adversier was finding this game amusing and said, "True, true. When you're right you're right. And this why you have to take our little trip on cloud nine. I don't want you to have another lighting bolt of compassion. It could be destructive to my plans. Of course, you won't be any good as a recruiter anymore. People always responded so well to you because they knew you cared. And now you won't."

Gabriella looked at all the faces surrounding her. She was looking for a remnant of the personalities she had known. It overwhelmed her when she saw none. "Yes and that's why they're all trapped here! All of you listen to me! If you know what we talked about in the meeting you know there is a way out for you. Ray, you don't have to take Liora anywhere. You can just let her go. You have a choice. Doctor, you can stop this right now. It doesn't have to go any further. No more people have to be destroyed."

The doctor was moved to his own defense. "A false accusation if I ever heard one. People aren't being killed by the Cloud Chamber. You are over-sentimentalizing the value of what is just a carbon copy. No matter how many copies of, let's say Ray, have their atoms scattered in the field. Ray is still safe and sound right here at the lab. The death of the team members came about because of these fear mongering Christians and their warped view of real life."

Gabriella challenged that statement by saying, "What about Joshua Cross and Lt. Harbinger? They survived the processing without being changed."

The professor responded as if they were just in a class somewhere on campus. "Ah, now you've proved my point. I admit I was stunned at first. Joshua should have been destroyed outright as the others were. I was trying to get rid of some City Council members and other civic leaders. Well, actually anyone who was in a position to block the lab's power expansion demands and other needs of the Project. These particular individuals only had an allegiance to their own plans and plots. Very much like myself but they couldn't be tempted by what I was offering. So I was forced to get rid of them. All I had to do was not have the receiver engaged and puff, 'ashes to ashes and dust to dust.' Joshua arrived earlier than expected, flung himself on the one person left and took the full beam. To my shock, they survived. It turned out they both had something in common."

Liora rejoined the fray with a flat statement. "They were both Christians."

Dr. Adversier's tone was patronizing when he said, "Yes, just like you my dear. Mr. Lewis was unconscious during this extraordinary turn of events so I just let him enjoy his wonderful escape from death. For a while any way. Unfortunately, Joshua took on an antagonistic attitude. Again, just like you my dear, and the late Lt. Harbinger. I offered them the abilities of a god! To be wherever they wanted to be, to do whatever they wanted to do. All they had to do was give up this insane obsession with life and eternity. It keeps them from really living here and now."

Liora tenaciously disputed his point. "You wanted them to give up Jesus. It was their relationship to Him that your machine couldn't overcome or change."

Gabriella decided to make another plea to the expressionless faces around them. "Look, I don't understand how or why their relationship with God short-circuits the effects of such overwhelming power. But I have seen that it does."

Liora quickly followed up. "Doctor, you and Ray, all of you, can be free from the changes this pseudo-pairing has done to you. Your body will die – it didn't survive the first transition to the inert state anyway.

But you can be paired with Jesus. In your own strength you can't stop doing the evil you've been doing. You'll just keep getting worse and worse. But you can be forgiven. In Christ you can regain the life you thought you'd lost. If you give up the body you can't keep anyway and allow Jesus to save you, His life will give you a life that will survive all this."

The argument irritated the doctor. Gabriella could hear it in his voice and see it in the look he gave Liora. "Yes, annoying human free will aligned with His will always has such unexpected side effects."

Adversier laughed out loud at that, as if he was very amused. He walked over to Ray and said, "I don't think Ray wants to die, do you Ray?" He gestured widely to the others and asked, "Or how about the rest of you? No answer? I didn't think so. I don't think they want to give up what they have for some over the rainbow promise."

He walked closer to Gabriella and contemptuously asked, "As for me, do you honestly believe I would use myself as a guinea pig? What I chose to be has nothing to do with science. I assure you everything I am is natural-or should I say supernatural. In their case, I saw the possibilities of a passive, inert human condensate who only moves when moved upon. Then I knew I had a counterpoint to God's turbulent entanglement with the human race. Odd how scientists miss it sometimes. When I first heard the word, 'entanglement' I thought that was it. It sounds like 'entrapment' and 'ensnarement' or, even better, 'enslavement'. But no, there's too much movement, energy and individuality. Now the 'condensate' had exactly what I wanted. It has the sound of being all light and sparkle, something I strive for myself. But with no sense of individuality and no independent action whatsoever. You'll find this interesting, Ms. Messenger. The process turns out to be a form of quantum anesthesia. The Quenching involves a massive depletion of light. So it interferes with those London Forces which are the bridge between the consciousness of the soul and the body. Like natural anesthesia, it turns off the same lever. It's a wonderful and unexpected side-effect."

Gabriella tried again to reach the impassive observers surrounding them. "Did you hear him? He's happy you are powerless inside your own body. Is that life? Is that what you are trying to protect? Are you alive at all? But did you listen to Liora's warning? She cares about you!" Gabriella yelled at them with her voice breaking at the end.

Full contempt was now visible on Adversier's face as he said, "I don't know how He stands you. If I had His power that lever would have been turned off long ago for every single one of you. And when I do...Get ready, Ms. Messenger, London bridge is falling down.

Wait...what is that sound? Shut up whoever is screaming immediately!"

Liora's eyes filled with tears and she struggled with the impassive Stan. No one in the Team had any reaction to the doctor's question. There had been no audible sound.

Dr. Adversier laughed. Then, whistling, he moved to the control console and switched on the Regeneration Beam. He turned to the Team and ordered, "Get our friend into the Chamber. Remember Gabby, there's only one way out of the Holy of Holies- dead or alive!"

Ray held Liora while Stan and Gil took hold of Gabriella. They started to move her toward the chamber which brought the three of them closer to the doctor. When Gabriella began to struggle Liora broke away from Ray, ran over and tried to interfere with the two first responders.

Dr. Adversier grabbed a hold of her and was pulling her away when she said tearfully, "Please, Vivi, stop. You're breaking Mom's heart."

"What!" said the professor, real emotion surfacing for a moment. "What did you call me? How did you know that name?"

Liora pulled a picture out of her lab coat pocket. It

was the same picture of a woman with the little boy and baby from her desk drawer. "This is a picture of you, me and Mom just before you were taken away by our father. She called you 'Vivi' because you were her 'vivid star', bright and brilliant. Don't you remember?"

Dr. Adversier stared at it for a second or two but then his eyes started blinking as if he was having trouble seeing. Suddenly he put his hand over his eyes, "Who's screaming again? Who's...no, no, impossible. My father told me my mother ran away with my sister and left me behind. You must have done your homework I have to say that. But your lies won't confuse me. Get Ms. Messenger into the chamber!"

Liora's voice became filled with desperation. "Please, brother, you're on the edge of the cliff and Satan is planning to push you off. Mom and I have always loved you. It took us years find out where you were. Whenever we'd get close our father would take off with you. He'd never allow himself, or you, to put down roots long enough for us to catch up. I came here to work in this lab so I'd have a chance to show how you were never forgotten and how you have always been loved by us and God. Vivi, please believe me now!"

"Stop!" Adversier shouted and then looked at Stan and Gil. "What are you waiting for! Get that woman into the Chamber!"

A sobbing Liora turned to Gabriella and said, "Rest in Jesus, Gabby! Rest, don't be afraid!" Then she called to the still impassive Ray saying, "Ray, don't let fear of death paralyze you. Dr. Adversier is paired with Satan. When they are done with you they can destroy this body and send you to Hell forever!"

Without warning, Ray ran over, grabbed Liora and pushed her away from Dr. Adversier. But, instead of restraining her, he took hold of the startled professor and began pulling him toward the Chamber. The strength of Adversier was amazing to Gabriella as she saw he was even pulling Ray with him in his attempt to re-acquire Liora. Stan and Gil's attention was now toward Adversier, as if awaiting an order. With the distraction Gabriella finally broke away from her captors and placed herself between Liora and Adversier. This again surprised the doctor but he made a sudden lunge and took hold of Gabriella. The loss of focus gave Ray the opportunity to finally drag the doctor into the Chamber. But the laughing Adversier had a virtual death grip on Gabriella so all three went into the Chamber together. There was an explosion of rainbow lights with a yellow wave band being transmitted out.

Liora hit the floor just as Peter, Angelique and Sean ran into the lab. "No!" Angelique cried out with Peter's "Gabby!"

Sean yelled for somebody, anybody, to "Turn if off! Turn it off!"

Liora was already back up and at the control and shut off the Regeneration Beam. There was silence and then – Gabriella stumbled out – alone. "My Lord. My Lord and My God!" she cried.

Liora ran to her, her sobs quenched by laughter almost hysterical with relief, and said, "You're saved!"

Sean, Angelique and Peter, also all laughing, joined the two of them.

Sean, after shaking Gabriella, said, "Where are the other two?"

Gabriella's laughter was quenched by the question. "Dr. Adversier was beamed out. Liora was there a receiver set up somewhere?"

Liora returned to the control panel, checked. Her tears had stopped but the pain was still in her voice when she said, "No. There was no other receiver for him."

Angelique voiced the question they all had when she asked, "And Ray?"

Gabriella smiled, a little sadly but with relief, and said, "He really helped save our lives. Somehow he heard and believed what we were saying."

Liora said, "He received Jesus and Jesus received him."

Sean smiled, nodded and turned to Gabriella. "And it looks like you did too."

Gabriella's whole face lit up with her smile. "In listening to Liora trying to convince the doctor and Ray that Jesus wanted to save their lives, and could save them even now, I was finally convinced myself." Reminded of what had just happened, she looked around and then asked, "Where's the rest of the Spectra Team?"

Everybody looked then and Angelique said, "Were they here? We didn't see them as we came in."

Peter walked over to several different spots in the lab and bent down. He said, "It looks like some of the Team came to the same conclusion you did, Gabby."

Liora asked, "But where are the rest?"

Sean had checked through the lab. "They've all scattered." And he added, "But where?"

Gabriella bent over as a wave of fatigue overwhelmed her. "That's a good question. But could we answer it another day?"

Angelique responded, "Sure. But can I ask how they got you here? We figured they took you from the parking lot since you left your car."

They had all been moving toward the door but Gabriella came to a sudden stop. "Now that's a question I'd also like the answer to. I remembered Liora might be in danger and rushed out the classroom door but I ended up rushing right through the door of the lab here."

Four pairs of eyes stared at her but Peter was the first to recover. "Man, biblical quantum transportation!"

"What!" was the only remark Gabriella could muster.

Peter launched into the explanation with, "Oh, that's something we didn't get a chance to tell you. There are a couple of examples in the Bible where it looks like the Lord may have transported someone to a location. You know, like a sudden quantum leap between location A and location B without passing through any points between." He was getting excited now and went on explaining. "Like Philip in Acts. The Ethiopian Eunuch was traveling on a desert road and reading what we know as Isaiah 55:7. He was wondering who this prophecy was about and why the one it described had to be 'led as a sheep to the slaughter.' He wished he had someone to explain it to him. The Lord told Philip to go to that road and to walk up to the Ethiopian's chariot without telling him why. He found out soon enough and was able to explain how the passage was referring to Jesus. After Philip's explanation the man accepted Jesus as his Savior and asked Philip to baptize him. Philip did and, as they came out of the water, the Bible states Philip was 'caught away' by the Spirit. He next found himself in a coastal city. The new believer didn't see Philip leave and Philip didn't know how he got to the coast. But he had delivered the message and the Eunuch took the message of the Gospel to Ethiopia."

Gabriella couldn't think of anything to say.

Peter said, "I'd say it's possible that the Lord answered several prayers by just getting you here - His way."

Gabriella said, "Peter, you're going to have to remember to mention little things like this," and then bent over laughing. "Wow, have I been drinking? But, I'll think about this later 'cause now, I'm kind of tired."

She staggered a little and Peter took her arm to help her keep standing. "No wonder, you've just discovered the most important message of your life. Come on Messenger. Let's get out of here!"

When the battle began both Net Man and the RGB Team had been in for a surprise. The Lamp exploded into full luminosity just as Net Man laid hold on her. At the same moment many of the Network surrounding them became a fleeting, illuminated incandescence flaring forth and then gone. Quantum Man's radiant energy flow had instantaneously tunneled through to parts of the Network and released them in a massive exchange of light and energy. They had allowed him in even though they knew their artificial lamps and colors would not survive the transition from unreality to reality. Only Quantum Man and Net Man knew the full power and effect of this exchange.

Although his Network was extensive and Net Man thought himself to be multi-present it was still only through those he controlled. Quantum Man was not so limited. While Net Man focused on one battle the war had been lost. Light Writer had given the signal and waves of the Full Spectrum had flowed out of Light Castles everywhere. As one they moved forward with joy into the benighted places. Like powerful rivers of living light they flowed around the dark fortresses until their deep darkness was overwhelmed with golden waves of glory and splendor crashing through their barriers. Many new Lamps were filled with light and the Light Castles shone even more brightly. Their expanding color range filled more and more of the dark world with Quantum Man's Full Light. Net Man decided to cut his loses, disperse the Network for now and disappear.

He had his plans. "So no great loss," he told himself. "There are still more of those Carbon Lamps wandering *around empty." He went off whistling in the dark and laughing in anticipation but he still didn't get it. "Well, it may be dark to him", Quantum Man said to the Full Spectrum. "But not to you." "Arise and shine," Light Writer wrote on their hearts. So they did and their darkness was like the noonday.*

Angelique, Sean and Peter had taken Liora and Gabriella back to Peter's house after a stop off to pick up Kitty from the Church. They had talked, eaten, prayed, cried and then laughed until the early hours of the morning. They knew they'd had a close call and a great victory. Angelique and Sean took Liora home, planning to stay with her until she didn't need them anymore. After they'd gone, Peter left Gabriella listening to some music while he looked at the story currently on his computer.

Peter had been experimenting with "Light Painting" as another way of doing the Quantum Man comic strip. He had created a series of images combining his on-going story, photographs and various light sources to create effects. On some light flowed like water. On others it exploded like a starburst. He watched the slideshow continuing to move the story through its paces. No wonder Adversier was nervous, he thought. Wow, Lord, You were putting his plans right out in plain sight for everyone to see. I wonder what will happen next?

Peter then remembered something he had wanted to tell Gabby.

"Hey Gabby, did I tell you I found another story Joshua had created. It has a character who is part of the Full Spectrum and does some special work for Quantum Man? She is known as 'Light Woman' but her alter ego name was Ariel Currier. Joshua had based it on this kid he knew of. He had already developed what she was going to do, why she was going to do it and where she was going on Quantum Man's behalf. But he never published it. His note just said it wasn't time yet. I thought now might be the time to do some stories on 'Light Woman'. What do you think?"

Since there was no answer he turned around and saw Gabby and Kitty peacefully asleep on the sofa. "You know, you guys have the right idea," he said. "I'll tell you tomorrow and, boy, will you be surprised." So he turned off the computer and went to bed. Gabby and Kitty didn't even notice.

Kathleen L. Daw

EPILOGUE

One of the schools devastated by Net Man and his Network had invited Professor Ariel Currier to become the new head of their Physics Department. While it would have normally been unheard of at her age her understanding of, and work with, light was now legendary. The Board had even thought about offering her the presidency of the college. But she refused both on the grounds she would be doing a lot of traveling. Instead, she had suggested the perfect person for the position of president. And someone who could effectively run the Physics Department as well. She would be away troubleshooting at other campuses. Both professors were known to be consistently "True Blue" and had accepted the assignments. So the school happily accepted of the arrangement. Freed from extra obligations, Professor Currier was often seen driving off with her faithful dog Kitty by her side. The Net had left many troubled campuses behind. But, in time, the darkness left behind by Net Man and his Net was lifting. Quantum Man made sure Light Woman and other members of the Full Spectrum Team went into every dark corner they could find and fill it with light. Light Writer said it was the Omega Attack and there was only One who knew how long it would take."

The alarm startled Peter but that was O.K. He knew he wouldn't be late as he grabbed his car keys and ran out. His note pad slipped to the floor and opened to the page where he had written:

Found a Thesis titled, "Measurement of the Tau Lifetime Using the ALEPH Detector." A. The Greek Tau is Tav in Hebrew. The Greek Alpha is Aleph in Hebrew. B. Genesis 1:1, "In the beginning God (ALEPH/TAV) created the heavens and the earth." C. Revelation 22:13 "I am the Aleph and the Tav, the beginning and the end, the first and the last." The Beginning measures the lifetime of the End. ALEPH/TAV is "ONE." The Tav was originally written as a cross. How about that! Check into it.

Angelique was standing outside the Mountain View Science Building. The spring temperature was brisk with a light breeze but the morning was bright and sunny. She was waiting to do the first of two stories which would be broadcast from the Campus today. She couldn't see the monitors in the van but she could hear all the instructions coming from Bob, the KCBC director, in her ear. Angelique knew when the audience at home would be seeing the most current picture of Dr. Lumière Adversier.

Now the director gave her the cue she was waiting for and the anchor launched into the story. "A nation-wide search is underway for the surviving members of the now discredited experimental Spectra Project."

As she was speaking the audience was looking at the video she had shot earlier in the day of the infamous and now deserted lab. Interviews with representatives from the Fire and Police Departments and the new head of the Mountain View Physics Department followed. Inter-cut with each interview were short clips of the Spectra Team.

The director gave her another cue and she was back live to finish up the story. "The scandal emerging after the death of Spectra Project Director, Lumière Adversier continues to widen in scope. Many related professions and industries were entangled in the project. It's expected to affect numerous careers."

She threw it back to Bob in the studio and left to cover the second story. One of the crew was coming to do most of the shooting on his own since she was also a participant in this particular event. Angelique left him with just a few instructions on what kind of shots she would need for the story. The director would also be monitoring the live feed from the camera. Any additional angles and changes could easily be requested.

The camera followed Angelique as she walked into a campus plaza surrounded by almond trees in all their white and rose spring glory. Looking around she found what she was looking for: Gabby, Sean and Peter. The three of them were immersed in kids and youth. The whole group was colorful enough to cast even the beautiful almond trees into the shade. The Quantum Man T-Shirts and baseball caps they were wearing were retro and reminiscent of the old Quantum Man T.V. show. In fact Angelique felt under dressed for the occasion until Peter put a cap on her head. It slightly messed up her professional and perfect hair but being included in the exuberant and enthusiastic group more than made up for it.

Gabriella was in total agreement. She, Sean and Angelique were there to support Peter and the big changes happening at Mountain View. They and the kids were honored guests and potential participants in the new Cross-Harbinger School for Gifted Children. It was being dedicated today at the Mountain View Institute of Technology. The school was both a return to the Institute's foundational roots and a revolutionary launching out into the development of future leaders. The curriculum combined the studies of theology, science and the arts.

Hearing his name announced, Peter, the keynote speaker, left them and stepped up to the podium. The large, supportive audience was made up of many who could hardly wait to get started on the future Peter was there to envision.

The joy he felt showed in the smile he beamed at everyone. "We are here today to dedicate a school in which science and the arts will flourish in the light of faith in God. That light will illuminate true artistic freedom of expression and a real understanding of the knowledge our scientific explorations bring to us. With Jesus, the Light of the World, within us we will raise up students who will walk boldly into the future. They will shine the light of revelation through the darkness which often obscures truth and reality. I'm speaking on behalf of the faculty of the Cross-Harbinger School for Gifted Children. We want these young students to receive true knowledge and understanding. We know if they see the Truth in us, they will come to know Him and He will set them free to bring His Light into every area of life. Along with dedicating this school today, I have also been given permission to make an announcement. The school motto is changed back to it's original statement which is Romans 12:7: *'We being many, are one body in Christ, And every one members one of another.'"*

Cheers and clapping erupted from the people who jumped up excitedly in front of Peter and around him. That included Gabriella. What a difference a year makes, Gabriella thought as she sat back down. Here I am actually overjoyed that my school is returning to the Lord who made it great. I'm wearing a Quantum Man T-shirt and happy about it. She probed her heart, looking for the familiar hurt, already sure she wouldn't find it. Joshua Cross would be thrilled to know how his influence had helped bring about this development. She laughed at the thought that he probably already did know. Then the light breeze of earlier in the morning quickly gained strength. Everyone around responded to the refreshing flow. Gabriella watched the colorful crowd moving about and talking enthusiastically with each other. They were like blossoms being stirred up by a strong wind.

Suddenly she heard the voice of her childhood's "Quantum Man" saying: "What is it like to be me?" the voice said. "Have you ever plunged through an emerald sea? Or flown through a sapphire blue sky soaring totally free? Felt yellow diamonds of glory pour over your head or washed in a river of fire from a love ruby red? Remember, the light that bounces back is from the angle you see and all those colors, and more, are what it's like to be me."

Her mind was about to supply the answer he had given so long ago when a voice in the crowd said, "Rainbow!" and all eyes turned to follow the hand that was pointing up.

In the sky above them was a circular rainbow.

Startled, Gabriella's mind immediately started to resurrect facts to fit the event. But then she stopped and closed her eyes. She felt as if she had plunged into a refreshing sea and yet was soaring totally free. Glory was pouring over her head and Love was washing her in a river of fire. She just whispered, "The answer is us in You, isn't it Jesus? Thank You, Lord."

Back at KCBC, the director had looked away from the camera feed for a few minutes to add to his notes. He wanted to ask Angelique to get interviews with Peter Lux and Gabriella Messenger. They knew a lot about how this stunning turnabout for the college had happened and he wanted an exclusive. When he looked back at the screen all he saw was a mass of swirling white and pink blossoms.

Pretty but useless he thought and then said, "Hey guys, can you get me another angle. I don't see any people at all."

The crew didn't immediately respond, which wasn't unusual. When they got caught up in one of these "artsy" shots it was like they weren't even on the planet. The blossoms look like they're dancing, was the next thought popping into his mind. Then he laughed and shook his head. I'm getting as bad as they are. He looked away and wrote down another programming note.

The two stood amid the swirling joy of the universe. In time it had been centuries, but truly He was back in no time and He was back as He had left. He was beginning as He was ending. A new heaven and a new earth was exploding out of the tomb. He was everywhere and there was no darkness. He and they were seeing as they and He were seen. He was here and they were there and here and there was joy, joy, joy! They witnessed it, they felt it and – finally – they understood it. They were ONE.

SOURCE MATERIAL

- The Holy Bible, various translations.

- Sermons of Dr. John Mastrogiovanni, 2007-2008.

- A Circle of Quiet by Madeleine L'Engle, 1972. Farrar, Straus and Giroux, New York, NY. ISBN: 0374123748. 246 pages.

- A Cry Like a Bell by Madeleine L'Engle, 1987, Crosswicks. Wheaton Library Series, Harold Shaw Publishers, Wheaton, Il. ISBN: 0877881480. 110 pages.

- Absolutely Awesome by Michael and Caroline Carroll, 1999. Tyndale House Publishers, Wheaton, IL. ISBN: 0842330437. 234 pages.

- A Guide to Weather by William J. Burroughs, Bob Crowder, Ted Robertson, Eleanor Vallier-Talbot, Richard Whitaker and with an introduction by John Zillman. 1996. Published by Fog City Press, San Francisco, CA. Printed in Thailand. ISBN: 978-1-877019-47-0. 288 pages.

- Angels: God's Secret Agents, Ringing Assurance that We are Not Alone by Billy Graham. Paperback: 288 pages. Publisher: Thomas Nelson; Reprint edition (June 26, 1995). 1975, 1986, 1994, 1995. ISBN-10: 0849938716, ISBN-13: 978-0849938719.

- Azusa Street: They Told Me Their Stories. The Youth and Children of Azusa Street Tell Their Stories Retold by Tom Welchel, 2008. Dare2Dream Books, Mustang, Oklahoma. ISBN: 0-9779688-0-4. 138 pages.

- Collins Dictionary of Physics: Physics Defined and Explained. Collins Internet-linked Dictionary of Physics by Eric Deeson. 2007. HarperCollins Publisher, Ltd. ISBN: 13 978-0-00-780082-7. 538 pages.

- Explorabook: A Kids' Science Museum in a Book by John Cassidy and The Exploratorium, 1991, Klutz, Palo Alto, CA. ISBN:1878257145. 100 pages.

- Exploring the Sky by Day: the Equinox Guide to Weather and the Atmosphere by Terence Dickinson. 1988. Fifth Printing, 1994. Camden House Publishing, Buffalo, NY and Firefly Books (USA) Inc., Buffalo, NY. ISBN: 0920656 (paperback). 72 pages.

- Genesis for Kids: Science Experiments that Show God's Power in Creation by Doug Lambier and Robert Stevenson, Illustrated by Ken Save, 1997, Lightwave Publishing Inc., Tommy Nelson, Thomas Nelson, Inc., Nashville, TN. ISBN: 0849940346. 159 pages.

- James Herriot's Animal Stories by James Herriot. 1997.The James Herroit Partnership. Michael Joseph Ltd., United Kingdom. St. Martin's Press, New York, NY. Printed in China. ISBN: 0-312-16874-8. 145 pages.

- Jesus and the Aleph-Bet, The Aleph and the Tav. Hebrew for Christians, Copyright John J. Parsons, All rights reserved. www.hebrew4christians.com

- Life is a Miracle: An Essay Against Modern Superstition by Wendell Berry, 2000, Counterpoint, Washington, D.C., ISBN:1582430586. 153 pages.

- Philip and the Ethiopian Eunuch, Acts 8:26-40, IVP New Testament Commentaries Resources Exegesis View, Bible Gateway. http://www.biblegateway.com/resources/commentaries/IVP -NT/Acts/Philip-Ethiopian-Eunuch.

- Philip Teleports? A Trivial Devotion. http://trivialdevotion.blogspot.com/2012/08/philip-teleports-acts-839-40.html

- Physics in the 20th Century by Curt Suplee, 1999. Edited by Judy R. Franz and John S. Rigden, American Institute of

Physics/American Physical Society. Publisher: Harry N. Abrams, Inc., New York, NY. ISBN: 0810990849 (Paperback edition). 223 pages.

- Quantum Physics and Theology: An Unexpected Kinship by John Polkinghorne, 2007, Yale University Press, New Haven, CT. ISBN: 9780300138405. 110 pages.

- Science and the Bible: Revised and Expanded by Henry M. Morris, 1986. Moody Press, Chicago. ISBN: 8616390. 154 pages.

- Scientific American, March 2008, Vol 298, No.3. Scientific American Inc., New York, NY. www.SciAm.com.
  - "Stirling in Deep Space: To Cut Back on Radioisotope Fuel, NASA Goes Back 200 Years" by Mark Wolverton, p.22.
  - "Here and There: Why Quantum Teleportation is Nothing Like Getting Beamed Up by Scotty" by J.R. Minkel, pp. 25-28.
  - "Voyagers to the End: The Solar System May be Dented at the Bottom" by Christina Reed, pp. 26-28.
  - "The Limits of Quantum Computers" by Scott Aaronson, pp. 62-69.

ABOUT THE AUTHOR

Born, raised and living in Southern California. Always writing since first learning how to hold a crayon. Poetry, plays, not very short e-mails to friends and stories with a cartoon character by the name of Pax have been the normal output of the author. This book is not in the normal category for the author but she prays it will become so.

www.ingramcontent.com/pod-product-compliance
Lightning Source LLC
Chambersburg PA
CBHW070815120626
46556CB00002B/518